D1029286

The Curse of Laguna Grande

The Curse of Laguna Grande

S. R. VAN ITERSON

Translation from the Dutch by Hilda van Stockum

WILLIAM MORROW AND COMPANY   NEW YORK 1973

Iterson, Siny Rose van.
    The curse of Laguna Grande.

    SUMMARY: A young boy in a remote area of Colombia tries to discover the circumstances surrounding his father's abduction many years before.
    Translation of Om de Laguna Grande.
    [1. Mystery stories. 2. Colombia–Fiction] I. Title.
I. Title.
PZ7.I9Cu   [Fic]   72–11469
ISBN 0–688–20071–0
ISBN 0–688–30071–5 (lib. ed.)

For Victor

The Curse of Laguna Grande

1

Everybody in the valley knew; that was certain. The farmhands who worked on the haciendas had told one another, and so had the people who lived in the hills around the great lake. The news had even reached the mountains at the other side of the Río Tigre, where Santos lived and the hut of El Cojo still stood.

Men discussed it in the little bar, Las Delicias, over their beer, but hesitatingly. They did not look one another in the eyes as they spoke. They twisted the sweating beer bottles between their coarse fingers and stared at the foam that frothed from the narrow necks.

"So that's the way it is," they muttered.

"Yes, that's the way it is."

"They're back."

"Yes, they're back at Payande."

"Have you seen them?"

"The jeep passed by here, just an hour ago."

"The jeep with the lady and the young master of Payande?"

"Yes, Juan de la Cruz went to fetch them from the village."

"So they're back, Ave María!"

"Yes, they're back at Payande." They fell silent. It was better to be silent about Payande. One never knew.

They ordered more beer. They talked about the sugarcane harvest, the cattle, and the accident that had happened at the Hollow Bridge. A long time ago there had been another accident there, ten years ago, perhaps longer. And now again. They muttered and fidgeted. They got up to go.

Blanca in her too tight red dress carefully counted the bottles. The men paid, walked slowly to their waiting horses, and swung themselves into their saddles. Each went his way: some along the narrow dark paths into the hills, some around the great lake or up the twisting trails leading to the mountains. Here and there someone stole a look at Payande.

Light burned there.

It was true. They were back!

It was good to be back in the old house, in the old familiar bedroom, in his own bed that had grown too narrow. It was good to lie there and listen to well-remembered sounds: the creaking of a rafter, the squeaking of a door somewhere in the house. From outside there came the heavy tread of the cattle in the dry grass, a rustling in the bushes. The wind wafted night echoes over the hills from the big lake, the Laguna Grande as the people called it.

The people were in awe of that lake. There it lay, dreaming among the hills. In the daytime it glittered in the sunlight. The tall old trees lining the shore threw cool shadows over the water. In the many inlets hundreds of water birds nested in the reeds. Early in the morning monkeys screeched in the wooded edges, and flights of raucous parrots skimmed the tops of the trees. In some places the lake had a lilac glow because of the small fields of water hyacinths that grew in it. And in the rainy season red, purple, and yellow flowers shimmered in the dark underbrush.

In the daylight it all looked friendly enough. But at night the lake had a mysterious quality. Then the dark water looked fathomless, the ink-black shore seemed full of wicked eyes and strange noises. Sometimes slightly phosphorescent flecks of light glowed between the reeds. Sometimes the water wrinkled as if a nameless creature stirred restlessly in its depths. Sometimes the lake was so still that one could hear the falling of a dry leaf or the rustling of a snake that had glided from a tree trunk into the water. Sometimes a fish splashed on the surface, only to dart away again between the hairy roots of water plants.

And sometimes, people said, the branches parted and a figure bent over the black mirror of the lake. Then a voice whispered, "Mine . . . all mine. . . ." and a reflected face wavered in the still water, too dark to be recognized. Only the reeds stirred, the old trees sighed, and the wind whispered over the water.

Sometimes even that was not heard. Then the night was filled with the dark call of frogs. Then each sound was drowned in the steady patter of the rain, for hours on end, on the wide expanse of the lake, on its wooded borders, on the waving grassland. It splashed on the mossy, tiled roofs of the old country houses and the straw roofs of small huts hidden among the hills. Then the water ran with silt and soil from the mountains. The thousands of small streams that crisscrossed the country overflowed their banks. Under the force of the oncoming water, rocks grated in the petrified bed of the Río Tigre, and the churned-up river roared with deep, dark growls. It was on such a night that his father had disappeared.

Carlos Arturo had been in his bed in the great dark room listening to the rain. The night appeared gray against the high windows. From afar came the roar of Río Tigre, and around the house the water pelted into the rain barrels. The dogs began to bark in the yard.

Then he heard hoofbeats and muffled voices. The barking stopped. That meant that the dogs had recognized the riders, that they weren't strangers.

A door opened and was shut again, the door of the study. Then came the sound of his father's heavy steps. His mother called something from their bedroom. The reassuring deep voice of his father answered her. Steps sounded in the hall, steps that receded.

Voices in the rain.

He slid out of bed and leaned far out the window. He hadn't been able to see anything. They must have been standing around the corner of the house, on the front square under the enormous shade trees. He heard the horses snorting and trampling the ground. For a moment he glimpsed the hindquarters of a horse, turning away. White hindquarters, shimmering in the rain.

The voices, the snorting of the horses, the rain falling in streams. Afterward the muffled rhythm of hoofs galloping off into the gray of the night.

He had remained listening until the sounds died away, until there was nothing to hear, except the rain. Shivering, he crawled back into bed, anxiously peering at the gray night outside the window. Tensely he listened for any sound in the rain. At last he fell asleep.

The next morning it was still raining, and in the house there was an uneasy strain. Don Raúl had not returned to Payande. First they waited, then they went to look for him. Hours went by, but they found no trace of him. Carlos Arturo never saw his father again.

His mother sat in the big hall without answering his questions. Transito, the old servant and house-keeper, walked around the verandas, wringing her hands. Sometimes she stood still in the front gallery, staring at the hoofmarks on the muddy front lawn.

"*Dios mío, Dios mío*," she whispered, horrified.

"Transito, what has happened?"

"How should I know?"

"Where is my father?"

"Your father! Ave María Purísima!"

"Who were those men?"

"Men?"

"There was one on a white horse."

"Hush! Be quiet. None of us saw anything."

In the kitchen the maids huddled together, and the farmhands, returning exhausted on sweating horses, stood in groups, muttering to each other. They fell silent when Carlos Arturo approached them.

The police were notified. Hundreds of people came to Payande: curious people, village notables, the mayor, the judge, and the doctor. Later the relatives, the city police, journalists, and soldiers came too. They searched the whole district for weeks. Everyone was questioned. But it was as Transito had said. No one had seen or heard anything. No one knew anything.

His mother, Doña Luisa, finally left for the city. His Uncle Ernesto, his mother's brother, took them to his grandmother's house. There they had lived for all these years, and for a while his grandmother's chauffeur had driven him to school.

The first months had been awful. The children stared curiously at him, and he felt that they whispered about him. The big city house oppressed him. His grandmother and Uncle Ernesto always stopped talking when he entered a room. His mother withdrew into her bedroom. He hardly saw her. Bent over his sums or in bed at night, staring into the darkness, he daydreamed about Payande and wondered why his father did not come to fetch him.

Gradually the images faded. Gradually he grew accustomed to life in the city, to the school rhythm, made friends among the boys. Payande became a distant dream.

And now, nearly seven years later, they had returned to Payande. All the images of the past assailed him now that he was back.

Back at Payande.

2

They had arrived in the little village late in the afternoon. The rattling wooden bus deposited them in the middle of the village square. There, under the spreading almond trees, it was already dusky and cool. A hog on a frayed rope rooted in the dry earth, and a lean dog slunk away into the shadows. The doors of the low houses stood open. Through their dark hallways glimmers of green were visible. Women and children stood in the doorways. They gazed after the bus, which was driving off in a cloud of dust. They watched the passengers scatter over the square, carrying bundles and bags. They peered curiously at the two, who remained standing awkwardly in the square.

Doña Luisa and Carlos Arturo looked around.

"Isn't Juan de la Cruz here to fetch us?" asked Carlos Arturo.

"I wrote and asked him to come," said his mother uncertainly. "But I don't see him."

A hubbub of voices came from the taproom of the gray, weathered hotel. In front of the small bars at the corners of the square stood saddled horses. Inside, in the small, dark rooms, men elbowed their way around the counters. Now and again someone peered out over the square at the figures of Doña Luisa and Carlos Arturo, who were still standing there in the shade of the almond trees.

"Is it them?" someone asked.

"Yes, *pues*. That's them."

"Then they've come back after all, Ave María!"

"Yes, I already heard. A few weeks ago. Doña Luisa wrote they were coming back to Payande."

"Who would have thought it . . . after so many years!"

"Yes, it was a long time ago . . . six years or perhaps seven. Time goes so fast."

"About six years."

"They never found him."

"No, they've never been able to find a trace of him. They searched the whole neighborhood, the villages and hamlets—no one knew anything."

"No, no one. Ave María Purísima!"

"Ah, it's better when you know nothing. You don't have to go looking for trouble."

"You said it!" They laughed and looked out at the two, who still stood there with their baggage under the almond trees.

In the taproom the notary and the doctor were having a drink together at a little table. The notary looked at the doctor and got up. The doctor, leaning his heavy body against the table and dreaming into his glass, paid no attention. He hadn't noticed Doña Luisa and Carlos Arturo in the square. The notary had and hastily left the noisy taproom, making a detour around the church to reach his shop. He was a small, fat man, and he stood still a moment in the wholesale liquor store to catch his breath. Then he walked with dignity through a dark hall to his office and his dusty papers.

"Are you sure Juan de la Cruz received your letter?" asked Carlos Arturo. "And did you tell him exactly the day we would arrive?"

"Yes, yes, I wrote it all. Several times. I don't understand it," said Doña Luisa vaguely. She looked around. "I asked Juan de la Cruz to come into the village with the jeep."

The shadows under the almond trees darkened. The narrow streets that ended in the square gaped hollowly. The lights went on one by one in the little bars and in the big taproom of the hotel.

"Shall I ask if someone has seen him?" Carlos Arturo suggested. His mother nodded hesitantly.

"Yes, you could do that."

Carlos Arturo sauntered across the square toward the houses and little shops. He felt that people were looking at him—curiously, or with aversion—and he walked as indifferently as he could. In a carpenter's workshop a solitary man was busy under the light of a naked bulb suspended from a long wire.

Carlos Arturo approached him. As he came near he saw that the man was working on a coffin. Long, unplaned planks stood against the wall.

"Good evening," said Carlos Arturo. The man stopped and looked at him.

"Good evening," he answered.

"We're from Payande," Carlos Arturo began. "We're waiting here for Juan de la Cruz. He was supposed to fetch us, but he hasn't turned up."

"Juan de la Cruz from Payande," repeated the man. He ran his hand along the rough wood of the coffin. "Juan de la Cruz seldom comes to the village anymore."

"He was supposed to fetch us, but I don't see him anywhere."

"No," said the man. "No, I haven't seen him either." He spat on the floor and went on with his work. Carlos Arturo threw an anxious look over his shoulder at his mother. He hesitated a moment. But the coffin maker went on with his work and didn't say anything more. Slowly Carlos Arturo walked back through the square, not knowing what to say to his mother or what to do next.

From one of the narrow side streets came the noise of an approaching car. A single headlight gleamed in the dark. A dusty, dilapidated jeep rattled into the square.

The jeep stopped. An old man with a lined face got out and hurried to Doña Luisa. He took off his sweat-stained hat.

"Juan de la Cruz," cried Doña Luisa. "How glad I am to see you. We've been waiting."

"How are you, *señora?* And young Señor Carlos Arturo? It's been a long time. . . . It's been a long time since the *señora* was at Payande." He began to load the baggage into the back of the car. They got in and rumbled through the square and the unpaved streets until they were out of the village.

"The road is bad," said Juan de la Cruz. "The road to Payande is bad, and the jeep is not much good anymore. They should fix the road, but you know how it is."

They drove over the darkening country road, which descended into the valley between the mountains. The one headlamp pierced the blue dusk.

"And how are things at Payande?"

"What shall I say, Doña Luisa? Things are well enough." His reply did not sound very convincing.

After a while he said, "It's been a long time since the *señora* was at Payande."

"Yes," said Doña Luisa. "Yes, it's been a long time."

"Don Ernesto, the *señora's* brother, has been here now and then. But always for a short time, never for more than a few days."

"That's right," agreed Doña Luisa. "It's a long journey all the way to Payande with those bad connections, and Don Ernesto has not much time. He is busy."

"No one has time in the big city," Juan de la Cruz said placidly. "The people all hurry, but they don't know where to. It's not the way it is here."

"How is your family? How are your wife and children?"

"The children are big now, and my wife is as usual, so-so. She's been ailing lately."

"What's the matter with her?"

"Always the same. Rheumatism and a light feeling in the head, she says. Sometimes she can't sleep with the pain."

"And the doctor, what does he say?"

"The doctor?"

"Doesn't she ever go to the doctor in the village with her complaints? Doesn't she get any medicine?"

"Ah, medicine. Yes, she goes regularly for medicine. But she remains sick."

"You could have brought her with you today."

"Yes, *señora*," said Juan de la Cruz meekly.

"And the children, how are they?"

"The boys are grown up. Only the youngest are still home. They help me, for it's hard to get workers on Payande. Only outsiders, from other places, will come, and they are seldom the best. There is always something to worry about. . . . And Carmencita, my daughter—the *señora* remembers Carmencita—is expecting her fifth."

"Carmencita? Yes, of course. I did not know she was married."

"That's how it is, *señora*. To Sabas, who lives on the *vaquería* and looks after the cattle."

"To Sabas?" repeated Doña Luisa. "To Sabas." She searched her memory. There used to be so many workers on Payande. "But Sabas used to live below, on Venetië, where the cattle graze. I thought he was married already."

"Yes, *señora*. But a few years ago his wife died. Sabas was left with a house full of kids and his mother, who is an invalid and can't walk."

"I see," Doña Luisa said with a sigh. "And now Carmencita has married him."

"That's the way it is, *señora*," repeated Juan de la Cruz.

They fell silent. The jeep bounced over the narrow road, ever farther into the valley. The vast, rolling landscape glimmered between the foothills of the mountains. The deeply cut dales were dark. There were thick borders of trees along the creeks and rivers, and the waving crowns of palms reached toward the millions of stars. The road made a sharp bend, and they drove through a dark green tunnel of shrubbery.

"Here comes Hollow Bridge," said Juan de la Cruz, slowing up.

"Hollow Bridge. . . ." Doña Luisa repeated automatically.

"Yes, Hollow Bridge." The jeep rattled over the wooden bridge. They could hear the water rushing over boulders in the shadows far below.

"The bridge where. . . ." Doña Luisa said uncertainly.

"That's it, *señora*. By this bridge. They've broadened it, but it's not much help. There was another accident here, not three weeks ago. Perhaps the *señora* heard of it?"

"How should I have heard of it. . . ?" Her voice was sharp. "Another accident?"

"The driver was a farmhand from Santa Barbara. He used to work on Payande. He drove off the side of the bridge."

"Off the side of the bridge," echoed Doña Luisa. "Off the side of the bridge . . . just like the other time."

"They say he was drunk," said Juan de la Cruz.

"But the people at Las Delicias say he wasn't there. They say they saw him pass as if the devil were at his heels." He was silent for a moment. "They talk so much," he added. He shifted gears. The road was mounting again. The beam of the one headlight illuminated another bend of the road and a big iron gate between weathered pillars, an overgrown wall, and thick shrubbery. Carlos Arturo gazed around him while the yellow light played over all. He was remembering.

"La Dorada," he said. "The gates of La Dorada."

"That's right." Juan de la Cruz nodded. "That's La Dorada."

"Don Belisario used to live there."

"He still does."

"We visited there. Don't you remember, Mother?"

"What?" asked Doña Luisa, startled. "What are you saying?"

"We used to go there, and I sometimes played with . . . with. . . ." He hesitated. He realized suddenly what a long time it had been since he had visited La Dorada with his parents. Faintly he remembered a great big white house with a tremendous lawn in front of it and a kind of well into which they had dropped pebbles. Or had that been somewhere else? He could not remember.

"I don't know," he ended uncertainly. "I thought we'd been there long ago."

His mother remained silent, and Juan de la Cruz said quickly, "The cattle on La Dorada are good, I hear. Not that I ever go there, of course. But Don Belisario keeps good stock there."

In the jeep, silence reigned. Carlos Arturo thought that Juan de la Cruz had been anxious to change the subject. But perhaps cattle and harvest were topics most familiar to him—those he knew best and could talk about.

Obviously his mother was tired. It had been an exhausting journey: first by plane, then by bus, and finally the long trip from the village to Payande in the jeep.

They almost had arrived, luckily. To the right he recognized the little bar, Las Delicias, with horses tethered in front of it. Groups of men stood inside drinking in the flickering light of a candle.

Now before them spread the broad landscape—rippling hills and dark valleys. Slender palms stood outlined against the fading sky. Far in the distance gleamed the lake, with its dark fringe of forest.

"There is the lake," exclaimed Carlos Arturo.

"Yes, that is Laguna Grande," echoed Juan de la Cruz.

"We're almost there!"

"Yes," said Doña Luisa, repressing a sigh. "We're almost there."

Good, thought Carlos Arturo. We're almost there

at last. Holding his breath, he peered intently along the road. "There!"

The iron gates between the pillars stood open. The driveway was overgrown with rank bougainvillea and poinsettias. Weeds grew between the stones. The jeep bounced through deep ruts to the front lawn. There lay the old house, deep in the shadow of the grand old trees. Its shutters sagged. Climbing plants grew over the weathered veranda. The mossy treads of the broad stone steps were cracked and crumbling.

A yellow light flooded one of the side porches. An old voice babbled, "Ah, *mi patrona*, ah, ah, ah. . . ." The grooved old face of Transito swam out of the yellow glow. "At last you are here. It is good to see you again at Payande, Doña Luisa . . . and the young master. So big he's grown!" She embraced Doña Luisa, she embraced Carlos Arturo, she wiped her eyes. Behind in the house there was shuffling and whispering. Faces appeared, then hastily ducked away again. The wife of Juan de la Cruz came forward, half bashfully, her sons following. Carmencita was there, the children hiding behind her skirts, and Sabas stood in the background, his hat clenched in his fists.

The trunks were carried inside. The old house gradually came to life. Doors were unlocked to the room of the *señora*, the room of the young master.

"The *señora* must excuse me," said Transito. The

flickering light of the oil lamps played over the large rooms, throwing grotesque shadows over cracked walls and dusty furniture.

Outside, far across the dark, still land, from the side of the lake, came the shrill cry of a night bird. They were back. They had returned to Payande.

3

They sat in the large dining room, his mother and he, each at a side of the long table. The tablecloth was yellowed, its creases too sharp. Outside it was already hot—a white heat. The cattle waded heavily through the dry grass on the hillsides. Small white herons tripped around on their awkward legs.

The doors and windows to the veranda were all open, but the rooms still held a musty smell. The smell of a house that hasn't been used for a long time, thought Carlos Arturo. He looked around. Nothing was changed, it was all as he remembered it, only older and shabbier. The upholstery of the furniture was threadbare. The legs of the table and big dresser were scratched and scarred. The walls showed damp spots, and cobwebs hung in the corners.

Carlos Arturo glanced at his mother. She looked

weary and was pale, with deep circles under her eyes. Her narrow hands played nervously with the folds in the tablecloth. Perhaps she was still tired after the long journey. Perhaps she had, like himself, been awake for the greater part of the night. Perhaps she also had been listening to the sounds in the dark and thinking of the past.

Transito entered, and behind her shuffled two bare-footed young servants in grimy dresses. They brought in the breakfast. Transito served the omelet and poured hot chocolate. She went around with warm *arepas*. The two servants stood and gaped at Doña Luisa and Carlos Arturo.

"Get on with it," snapped Transito impatiently. "Where is the fruit juice? You've forgotten the glasses of fruit juice! The *señora* must excuse me," she said in the same breath. "Those girls are new. They know nothing. They are stupid, and I haven't been able to teach them anything. It's difficult to get help. Most of them. . . ." She stopped, as if frightened.

"Yes," said Doña Luisa absently. Her nervous fingers crumbled an *arepa*. Her glance traveled over the two girls, who stood there, awkward and mute, with dull, expressionless faces.

"Tell them at least to wash their hands," she said to Transito. "Or perhaps it would be better if they didn't serve at the table at all."

"Yes. And then there is the matter of the light," continued Transito. "The generator won't go anymore. Juan de la Cruz has tried everything, and he doesn't know what to do, he says. But I hope the *señora* had a good night, at least."

"It could have been better." Doña Luisa smiled. "The road was very bad."

"Yes, the road is bad," agreed Transito. "But the *señora* is lucky that the rainy season hasn't started yet. When the rain begins, Ave María. The *señora* knows."

She took the two glasses with fruit juice from the tray that one of the girls had fetched finally. Carlos Arturo ate hastily, hunched over his plate. He did not want to look at his mother, who seemed ill at ease, playing absently with the glass, from which she did not drink. He felt uncomfortable too. The homecoming was very different from what he had imagined.

He had been so happy when his mother told him that they were returning to Payande—Payande, the big hacienda where he had spent his childhood, with its wide, rolling pastureland, its numerous little rivers edged with dark woods, the great old house bustling with life, where there always had been something to do. He remembered the stories the maids and farmhands had told him of the great haciendas in the neighborhood and the people who lived in the hills around Laguna Grande. How often he had been homesick when he still lived with his grandmother. He never had felt at home with her, as if they were only visiting —and really they were.

At the time moving in with his mother's family had been the only solution. The hacienda was their sole source of income, and the business end of it had grown steadily worse. There were debts to the bank, the harvest yielded less every year, the cattle dwindled. Carlos Arturo caught a word here and there when his mother and Uncle Ernesto discussed these things. Uncle Ernesto occasionally had traveled to Payande. His mother had not accompanied him, however, and Carlos Arturo was not allowed to go either, not even during his vacations. His uncle never stayed long. Not long enough, thought Carlos Arturo, to inspect the land or to appraise the cattle. And always, when his uncle returned, his mother had been irritable and unhappy, avoiding his questions about Payande. In the beginning he did not realize it, but when he grew older, he suspected that they were keeping things from him. So he had been happy when his mother told him that they were going to live at Payande again, that the estate must, somehow or another, be made productive. They could not keep on living off the family.

Carlos Arturo realized that most of the responsibility would fall on his own shoulders, but he welcomed that. He knew every bit of the land; he knew its people.

Payande was part of him. And yet, as he sat there that first morning, the house seemed unfamiliar to him. No murmur of voices in the kitchens and the outbuildings, no walking to and fro, no bustle of activity. And those strange, new servants who kept staring at him! With a jerk he shoved his chair back when he saw his mother getting ready to rise.

"I'm going to walk around for a bit," he said. He received no answer. When he left the hall, his mother was standing by the long table, looking forlorn.

Slowly he sauntered through the large rooms, through the broad passages, across the many patios. This house where he had lived for so long, where he hadn't been for so long, was familiar and yet strange.

The furniture occupied the same old places. Enormous sofas whose silk covers were worn. Wood attacked by termites. Traces of rats and mice near holes in the floors. The old family portraits in black frames hanging crookedly. The plaster flaking from one of the ceilings. Cracks and moldy spots everywhere.

On either side of the door leading into the small hall stood a huge painted vase holding a bunch of peacock feathers, which, as a child, he always had called the "blue palms." In the guest rooms the torn mosquito netting had been hoisted to the ceilings. The mattresses smelled damp, and the mirrors of the enormous wardrobes were flyspecked.

34

He wandered farther and farther through open galleries where great stone cisterns stood, spotted with green, and old-fashioned tables and chairs covered with cowhide. In the patios grass grew between the flagstones. The plants in the alabaster flowerpots had withered. In the center of a small, sunny patio stood a mermaid of green porcelain, gasping for breath in a dry fountain.

He sat down for a moment on the warm edge of the fountain. There was so much that he almost had forgotten and now suddenly recognized again. The little mermaid, for instance. How often had he sat there and watched the goldfish glide between her raised arms in continuous and everchanging play. Now the graceful gesture had hardened into a meaningless pose. Nothing was really changed, and yet Payande was no longer the home of his childhood. It had become lonely, lifeless, petrified, like the gesture of the little mermaid.

He got up and went on without enthusiasm, following a rough path that led to a little colonial chapel. Its white walls were covered with tender pink blossoms, but the windows were black and cobwebby, and the door was locked.

Half hidden behind the chapel stood a small building. Its door was open. He saw a big table in the middle of the room and along the walls deep cupboards full of dusty bottles and boxes with medicines and pills, long dried up and useless. A glass cupboard contained old instruments: scissors and hypodermic needles. Outside against the wall was a bench. He remembered that this small dispensary had been a hobby of his father and that his mother had never liked it when he had asked her to help him with the distribution of the medicines or the giving of injections.

He wandered farther along the outbuildings and sheds, and then slowly returned to the big house. There was one room he had not visited yet. He stood hesitating a moment before its closed door. All at once he was overcome with the feeling he used to know, a certain fear of entering his father's study.

He opened the door and went inside. It was quiet there and half dark. The familiar musty smell met him. The shutters were all closed. Tendrils of wild vines entered through cracks and slits. He pushed open the shutters, and the green sunlight cast whirling stripes of dust into the room. His glance skimmed the familiar furniture, the worn leather chairs, the big table in the middle, and the high bookcases against the walls. Rows of dusty books, some nibbled at by cockroaches and ants, some falling apart from the damp, stood on their shelves. A few rows of leatherbound classics seemed still intact. Tucked in a corner were a row of textbooks and yellowed notebooks from his father's student days.

Two saddles, their leather hardened, lay on trestles

against the wall, and above them hung a headpiece and spurs. A big bull's head had been fastened on the wall beside the door, and from one of its horns hung an old straw hat.

Carlos Arturo looked for a long time at the hat, so carelessly dangling there as if its owner might come any moment. Slowly he withdrew his gaze, walked to the great curved desk, and sat down behind it in his father's old chair.

He pulled out the drawers of the desk one by one and began to look through the stacks of papers and documents, sorting them out. Account books, notations about the cattle, old bills, correspondence. In one of the drawers, between letters and paid bills, he found an envelope with photographs. He pushed aside the papers and let the prints slip through his hands. A few had been taken at the *vaquería*, Venetië. They showed an enormous zebu bull with a flabby hump and pendulous ears. Grouped around him, all on horseback, were his father, he himself, a heavyset man in a checked shirt whom he did not recognize, and Sabas on a little brown mottled horse. In the background were the shadowy faces of a few of Sabas's children, who had scrambled into the picture. There were several of these prints, each posed a little differently, but obviously the big, beautiful zebu bull had been the reason for the pictures.

The other snaps had been taken on the veranda of

the house, probably to finish the roll of film, thought Carlos Arturo. He was looking wistfully at the group on the veranda: his father, his mother, the big man in the checked shirt, and two other gentlemen, one of whom he vaguely remembered as mayor of the village. In one of the pictures he saw himself leaning against his father's chair, and in one he was alone. He deduced that the photographs had been taken shortly before they left Payande. Perhaps they were the last photographs of his father.

He put the envelope back and shut the drawer. Abstractedly he opened the next one. His attention had wandered. He sat staring at the copy of an act of sale without realizing what it was, when his mother entered.

"Oh, here you are," she said.

He did not answer.

"What are you doing?"

"Nothing. I'm just looking."

She noticed the open drawer and the papers lying on the desk.

"There's so much to check over," he said.

"Yes, there's a lot. A whole lifetime."

"It will be a while before I have everything straightened out."

"Let me have a look." She took him by the shoulders and pushed him gently away, putting the papers back in the drawer. Then she began, as he had done, to go through the desk systematically, starting with the top drawers.

I hope she doesn't find the photographs, Carlos Arturo thought. But he knew that inevitably she would. He wished now that he had not put them back. He did not want to be present when she found them, and he had the feeling that she was not very pleased to have him watch what she was doing. Suddenly he felt superfluous and left the room as unobtrusively as possible. At the door to the kitchen he saw Transito talking to Juan de la Cruz, who was wiping a black, oil-stained hand over his face.

"It's that generator," he was saying in a discouraged tone. "I can't start the motor. Everything has rusted. I'll have to tell the *señora*. I've been tinkering with it for days, but it won't go. The *señora* won't like it when there are no electric lights this evening."

"There is the matter of the servants too," said Transito with a sigh. "I saw this morning that the *señora* did not like them. But I can't help it. No one in the neighborhood would come here. I had trouble enough to get these girls. You know how it is."

"Yes," Juan de la Cruz agreed. He nodded thoughtfully. "That's the way it is. It's difficult. People don't like to come after what happened."

"True." Transito threw a warning glance at Juan de

39

la Cruz. "It's better if we don't. . . ." They looked around nervously and were startled to see Carlos Arturo.

"What is it? What are you talking about?"

Juan de la Cruz tipped his hat. "It's the generator for the electric light and water," he answered. "I can't start the motor. It's stubborn. I wanted to tell Doña Luisa."

"My mother is in the office," said Carlos Arturo. Juan de la Cruz always had called his father's study the office.

"Ah, there," said Juan de la Cruz and shuffled off rapidly toward the study.

"What were you talking about just now, Transito?" asked Carlos Arturo again, when he was alone with Transito. Transito sighed deeply.

"I don't know what to say, Master Carlos Arturo," she muttered, wiping a wrinkled hand over her sunken mouth. "I don't know what to say. Things are not what they used to be, and that's the truth." She shook her old head sadly. "No, things are not what they used to be," she repeated softly.

4

No, things are not what they used to be, thought Carlos Arturo bitterly, as he rode over the estate the following days. In the six, nearly seven years that they had lived in the city, the big hacienda that had been in the family for three generations had gone downhill rapidly.

The big house was dilapidated. Old Transito and the two new maids had their hands full, straightening it out. And as for the men who were working on the land, Carlos Arturo didn't know a single one of them. They were not from the neighborhood, as Juan de la Cruz had told him. They did not work hard; that was obvious. Juan de la Cruz had no control over them, neither had his two sons. Carlos Arturo saw that he would have to take charge. But doing so would be difficult. There was so much to learn all at once!

The enormous herd of cattle they once had owned had dwindled to almost nothing. The land looked poor

. . . the land! That was the worst, thought Carlos Arturo. The land where valleys, trails, and rivers all brought memories of his father. Together they had fished in the many streams and swum in the deep pool between the big stones in the Río Tigre. Sometimes they had gone to Laguna Grande, but Carlos Arturo had not liked the big lake. It always had frightened him. They had hunted in the hills; they had ridden on horseback to count the cattle and survey the harvest. The harvest!

Carlos Arturo rode thoughtfully down a narrow path between high sugarcane. At a turning in the path he encountered a group of men cutting the cane.

"I didn't know you were working here," said Carlos Arturo. "This morning I told Juan de la Cruz that you were to go to El Piñal at the other side of the river."

The men stopped working and looked at one another. They muttered something and fell silent. At last one of them said, "Well, we were sent here this morning."

"Sent here? Who sent you?"

"The foreman of Santa Barbara."

"The foreman of Santa Barbara?" echoed Carlos Arturo. "How can that be?"

"Well," said the spokesman, tilting his hat to the back of his head, "we work on Santa Barbara, and the foreman sent us to cut sugarcane."

"But this land does not belong to Santa Barbara,"

Carlos Arturo exclaimed impatiently. "It belongs to Payande."

"I don't know, *señor*. We were sent here by the foreman." Shrugging his shoulders, the man began to cut again.

Carlos Arturo rode on. How could workers from Santa Barbara be cutting sugarcane on his land! Did his mother know? Or Doña Isabel, the owner of Santa Barbara?

Slowly he rode toward Santa Barbara, his mouth tight. Santa Barbara, the great prosperous estate with its many workers, its gleaming cattle, and its extensive sugarcane fields. Santa Barbara, with its long, low, white plantation house sitting proudly on a hill in the center of the land, the house with the tower! There, in that house, lived Doña Isabel. She had lived there for years, absolutely alone. And she managed to keep things going. Why hadn't his mother managed? Why had she left Payande? Why didn't the men want to work on Payande anymore? Why were they afraid?

What had happened to his father that night? Who were the men that had come to fetch him? Men who came on a dark rainy night. One on a white horse!

Why had his mother never wanted to talk about the tragedy with him? Was she afraid too, like the others? Why? Always why? Why hadn't his mother stayed with him on Payande? Like Doña Isabel on Santa Barbara.

Why could Doña Isabel do what my mother couldn't? thought Carlos Arturo bitterly. What powers had Doña Isabel over her workers, her land, her cattle?

She never showed herself. Even before, when they had lived at Payande, he seldom had seen her. She never went to inspect her possessions, count her cattle, survey her harvest. Never. But every year the sugar-cane stood high and green along the banks of the Río Tigre. Every year the cattle increased. Every year was better than the one before for Santa Barbara. And for Payande? Now the workers of Santa Barbara were harvesting Payande's land. Carlos Arturo felt a burning hatred flame in him. He hated her, he hated Doña Isabel in her white plantation house on the hill, the house with the tower!

His father used to tell him about that house. Santa Barbara was the oldest hacienda in the region, dating from the time of the Spaniards. It was older than Payande and older than La Dorada where Don Belisario lived. Much older. In the course of time many legends had been woven around the house. Its inhabitants were supposed to be invulnerable. During the battle for liberty in the last century when the house had been besieged by patriots, the Spanish general who lived there had managed to escape unharmed with his family. No one knew how, but that's what people said. His father had told him also. Could a house confer power on its inhabitants? Could Doña Isabel for that reason . . . ? He did not know. He turned his horse, riding slowly home. He must talk over the matter with his mother. But she was so vague and reserved! And she did not love Payande, not as he did, or as his father. . . .

No, he must not keep thinking of his father. That didn't help. He had to try and solve the problems himself. But doing so was difficult!

He descended into the valley where the cattle grazed, the region called Venetië. The fields were crisscrossed by streams coming from the mountains. It was cool in the shadow of the trees that edged them. The cattle grazed in pairs in the long grass. From the thick shrubbery along one of the creeks he heard the bleating of a very young calf. He dismounted. Leading his horse, he began to search among the bushes. A lean cow suddenly broke through the branches and dashed past him, just missing him.

"Ah!" Carlos Arturo heard a voice say. He waded through the high grass in the direction that the cow had gone and discovered Sabas, the head cowhand. Sabas stood hidden in the shadows of the bushes. With his hands in front of his lips he made a trembling, mournful noise, exactly like the bleating of a very young calf. The lean cow ran nervously through the long grass and then stopped, snorting, head bent.

"Ah," repeated Sabas. "Just as I thought." He looked

at Carlos Arturo and then at the small cow. "Early this morning I thought she had calved, and now she has brought me to it."

Watching the nervous mother cow, they went to the place where the little calf lay hidden among grass and bushes.

"It's a good calf as far as I can see," said Sabas.

"Yes, it's a good calf," agreed Carlos Arturo.

They mounted, riding among the cattle.

"Soon we'll have to count them," Carlos Arturo remarked.

"Yes, *señor*," said Sabas.

"And the young animals must be branded."

"Yes, *señor*."

"Many of the fences are broken."

"Yes, *señor*."

"We'll have to do something about them."

"Yes, *señor*, but there is no more barbed wire, and we haven't got any posts either."

"I'll remember when we go to the village," said Carlos Arturo. "I can buy the wire there. We used to cut the posts ourselves in the quarries."

Sabas kept silent, and Carlos Arturo asked, "How are things at home?"

"So, so," mumbled Sabas. "My first wife died, and my mother is not well. Always the same. It's her hips. She can't walk; she just sits there."

"I'll pass by and say hello," promised Carlos Arturo as he left.

On the way home he met some of Sabas's sons, who were rounding up cattle with loud cries. They lifted their hats when they saw him. Carlos Arturo talked to them for a while, and then watched them gallop off over the fields on their tough little horses.

Sabas's home was located between two narrow creeks. It was a big wooden house with a wide veranda. A group of children played in the shabby yard among the hogs and chickens. They fled into the house when they saw him, and the dogs barked.

A moment later Carmencita, who was now Sabas's wife, appeared in the doorway. She carried a little girl, and under her brown arm her childish young body was swollen. Two bigger children hung on her skirts. One tried to grab her free hand.

The old mother sat on the wide wooden veranda in the shade of the protruding roof. She hunched crookedly in a rough, leather-covered wooden chair and stared at Carlos Arturo. "Who is that?" she called to her daughter-in-law impatiently, when Carmencita shyly approached Carlos Arturo and greeted him.

"It is Señor Carlos Arturo, ma'am," Carmencita answered. "From the big house, from Payande. . . ."

Carlos Arturo dismounted and went to the old woman.

"From Payande," echoed the old woman pettishly. "From Payande."

"Please come in," said Carmencita hastily. She preceded him, still a child, with angular dirty knees under her tight, faded dress. The little ones stuck close to her, the smallest on her arm.

Inside it was dim and cool. Hammocks had been hoisted to the ceiling. In a corner a green parrot shrieked. A couple of lanky boys, sons of Sabas, hastily disappeared, and Carmencita chased a chicken from the table and fanned away the flies that hummed around the jug of *panela* water.

She poured Carlos Arturo a glassful of the tepid brown fluid. "You'll have something to drink, won't you?" she asked shyly. Carlos Arturo nodded. He emptied his glass in one draft.

"It's warm," he said.

"Yes, it's warm," affirmed Carmencita. They fell silent. Outside, on the veranda, the old woman coughed and wheezed.

"And how is the *señora*, your mother?" asked Carmencita.

"Unsettled still," said Carlos Arturo. He added without thinking, "The house is very run-down, and so is the land and the cattle. Much will have to be done."

"Yes," said Carmencita. "My father has done what he could, and Sabas too. *Señor* knows that I am married to Sabas now."

"Sabas! What do you say about Sabas? Sabas is a good son, a very good son!" the old woman called from the veranda. They heard her thick shapeless body shift about in the clumsy chair. "What are you saying about Sabas, Carmencita? Sabas is a good boy!"

"Yes, ma'am," Carmencita answered obediently. She looked furtively at Carlos Arturo.

"Now that Doña Luisa and Don Carlos Arturo are back again, we'd like to leave. Perhaps Sabas has told you already," she said hesitantly.

"Leave?" asked Carlos Arturo, shocked. "Leave? Where to?"

"We want to go to the city."

"To the city? But Sabas has always lived here, and he's the only one who knows the cattle. What does Sabas want to do in the city?"

"We want to go to the city," repeated Carmencita in the tone of a child who has learned something by heart that she does not really understand. She began to stroke the rough top of the table. Now and again she glanced nervously at the doorway.

Outside the old woman was muttering, "There is nothing to say against him. He has always been good to his mother. He is a good boy."

"She isn't all there," whispered Carmencita nervously. "She doesn't always know what she is saying. She is very old." She kept stroking the tabletop. Carlos Arturo watched her.

Plainly Carmencita was ill at ease. Was she afraid? Afraid of the ailing old woman who bullied her? Perhaps afraid of Sabas, who was so much older, who had grown-up sons already? Or had she been frightened by his sudden visit? Perhaps he had offended her by mentioning that the house was dilapidated and that much work had to be done. There was no telling. The conversation had been fragmentary and stilted. Not the way his father, who was always making jokes, had talked with his people.

What would Sabas, who had grown up in the country, do in the city with his large family? And what would he himself do on the *vaquería* without Sabas? Sabas who knew everything about cattle and who could imitate a newborn calf well enough to deceive its own mother!

The old woman on the porch began again to call impatiently, "Carmencita!"

Carlos Arturo rose hastily. "Sabas has not yet told me that he wants to leave," he said. "You'd better think it over for a while."

"Yes, *señor*," said Carmencita politely. But Carlos Arturo understood that they had decided to leave.

5

"If the *señora* wants to go to the village, she shouldn't wait too long," said Juan de la Cruz. "When the rainy season starts and the rivers begin to swell. . . ."

"Yes," said Doña Luisa. She nodded absently. To herself she thought, There is so much to do here that I can't leave. But it will have to be done. I must. . . .

"And we need new parts for the motor," said Juan da la Cruz. "I tried everything, but I can't start it. The *señora* must have electric light."

"Yes," agreed Doña Luisa. "Those oil lamps are such trouble."

"That is so." Juan de la Cruz nodded. He remained standing, hat in hand. "And when the rains begin presently . . . the road is bad as it is, and the bridge isn't safe. The *señora* has surely noticed. There was an accident there again, not so long ago."

"So you said," murmured Doña Luisa.

"No one knows how it happened," Juan de la Cruz continued. "They found him the next morning, and then it was too late to do anything. They called Ana-Amanda, but there was nothing to be done."

Carlos Arturo, who stood on the veranda looking out over the fields, half turned. "Ana-Amanda," he repeated. "Ana-Amanda, is she still alive?"

"Certainly, certainly," Juan de la Cruz assured him. "What would we do without her?" He cast a timid glance at Doña Luisa, but Transito had just entered and she wasn't paying attention.

"Ana-Amanda still lives in her hut among the rocks at the other side of the lake. She still goes searching for herbs. Yesterday I saw her. She sends greetings to your family. She says she is always at your service."

Carlos Arturo gazed at the great lake lying between its wooded shores. Many paths crossed the rolling land, where small huts hid among the greenery of bananas and corn. How often he had followed those paths on horseback beside his father! Nearly always they stopped somewhere and had a chat with the inhabitants. His father knew all the people living around the great lake.

"Well, Gloria," he might call out, "how are you? What's new?" The young woman came hastily to the road, the children and dogs trailing her.

"What shall I say, *señor?* My little boy is ill, the one who is not a year old yet."

"What's the matter with him?"

"I don't know, *señor.* He just lies there and cries all the time. And he won't eat. He throws up everything." She motioned toward the hut, and Don Raúl rode into her yard. In the doorway of the hut a little boy, who was whining, sat in a crate. In the darkness of the hut one of the older children was hushing a newborn baby. Don Raúl dismounted and bent over by the crate. The child, dressed in a short shirt under which his belly bulged, kept on crying. Saliva dribbled from his open mouth. The mother wiped it off with a smelly rag that was lying in the crate.

"It's because I took him with me when my husband's sister was dying. He caught her illness. The chill of death has come over him, Ave María." She sighed and once more wiped the dirty face with the smelly rag.

Don Raúl shook his head. "He probably has got worms. Have you no clean towel? You must use water and soap. Wash him, Gloria, and wash the little baby there too."

"Yes, *señor.*"

"This afternoon or tomorrow you may come to Payande. We'll have a look at him and give you some medicine."

"Yes *señor*," Gloria said again. But she would not

come. She would wait passively, and if the child got worse she would go to Ana-Amanda, in her hut among the rocks, and she would go when the moon was waning.

Ana-Amanda was a very old woman. A *bruja*, a woman who made healing potions out of herbs and the juices and roots of plants, or from the fat of iguanas and the slime of snakes and frogs. She made trees bleed, and then caught the white sap in a bottle without a neck.

Everyone in the neighborhood knew Ana-Amanda. Many asked for her help when they were in trouble, as when a man was brought home wounded after a fight, which happened often, or when a child was ill, which also happened often. They always brought an offering despite their poverty: a piece of *panela*, or a candle, a few eggs, or even a whole chicken. It was rumored that if they had absolutely nothing to give, Ana-Amanda let them work for her. Carlos Arturo couldn't imagine what kind of work Ana-Amanda needed done in her simple hut behind the lake.

He always had been scared of the old woman and of the place where she lived—scared but also fascinated. He sensed that his father disapproved of Ana-Amanda's practices and knew that sometimes his father warned her to stop them when she went too far. Once, for example, they had found a child buried in a hole filled with cow's dung. "To chase the chill of death," the

54

mother explained. Only the head of the child with its big, frightened eyes stuck out of the earth.

But the people believed in Ana-Amanda and talked about her with awe. Her power was great. A labyrinth of footpaths led to her hut among the rocks.

It leaned against a huge rock wall called the stone ridge. It was dark and damp there. In the yard grew weird shrubs with pink, cuplike flowers that had a bad smell. Turtles crawled there, armadillos and rabbits hid in the bushes, and a great screeching parrot sometimes hopped about on the edge of the sagging door. Iguanas with pulsing throats sat on enormous boulders that were scattered around the yard. Everything in that unreal world, where bitter smoke drifted from great black caldrons, was gloomy and uncanny.

Ana-Amanda, withdrawn and taciturn, busy with her animals and herbs, was always dressed in black—a long black gown and a man's black hat. She was a proud woman, who almost never spoke if not spoken to. She wandered about searching for herbs in the hills, in the mountains, and along the marshy banks of the lake. Most people dreaded the lake. They talked about it with awe and barely concealed fear, much as they talked about Ana-Amanda.

"Did she say anything?" Transito used to ask, when she knew that Carlos Arturo had been to Ana-Amanda with his father.

"Who?" Carlos Arturo would ask evasively.

"Ana-Amanda."

"No, what would she be saying?"

"She didn't say anything special, about someone in the neighborhood, for instance?"

"No, I don't think so."

"That's all right then," Transito would answer, sighing with relief and a slightly letdown feeling.

It had been a long time before Carlos Arturo understood what Transito was getting at with these questions. Slowly he began to realize that whenever Ana-Amanda made a remark about something or someone, it came true. She would prophesy a bad harvest or an illness among the cattle. She had predicted the flood that happened years ago and also the day that all the fish in Laguna Grande had come floating belly up . . . dead. She might look at someone, shaking her head a little, and warn him that he had better take care, he would not live much longer.

Only my father's death, thought Carlos Arturo. That she did not foresee, or she would have said something. He kept staring at the big lake in the distance, his hands clutching the railing of the veranda. Then he remembered that El Cojo had been the one who had warned his father.

6

"Look," said Transito. She made a movement with her chin toward the dusty road. "There they go with the pickup to Santa Barbara. It must have been repaired."

Carlos Arturo looked in the indicated direction. Yes, there went the pickup in a cloud of dust.

"Is that the car that had the accident at Hollow Bridge?"

Transito nodded her old bird's head. "Yes, that's the car Edelio was driving. It was badly damaged. They had it repaired, but poor Edelio!"

"It's a dangerous place, the bend in the road and that narrow bridge with no railings."

"It was near his house. They didn't find him until the next day. Dear Lord, you never know where you may end up dead."

"They called Ana-Amanda, didn't they?" said Carlos Arturo.

Transito nodded. "Yes, they did. But there was nothing to be done. Ana-Amanda knew about the accident already when they came to fetch her. She is very old and very wise and occupies herself with things that ordinary folk don't understand."

"Juan de la Cruz told me that Edelio used to work on Payande."

"A long time ago," said Transito. "Recently Edelio was working on Santa Barbara. The old lady, Doña Isabel, was quite upset when she heard about the accident." Transito sat down on a chair near the kitchen table.

"Have you seen her yet?" she asked. "Have you visited her?"

"Who?"

"The old lady, Doña Isabel, at Santa Barbara."

"No, I haven't been to Santa Barbara yet," Carlos Arturo answered. There was aversion in his voice, but it escaped Transito.

"You should go to her. You should visit Doña Isabel now that you are back. She is getting old, and she was always very fond of your father." Transito nodded to underline her words. "Yes, she was very fond of your father. When Don Humberto, Doña Isabel's husband, and their daughter María Teresa still lived, the families saw a lot of each other. I think Don Humberto and Doña Isabel would have liked María Teresa to have married your father. Yes, I'm sure of it. The families were great friends, and your father and María Teresa were always together when they were children. I believe that Doña Isabel would have been pleased if Santa Barbara and Payande had come under one management. But you know how those things are. . . . Your father went to the city to study, and María Teresa remained behind on Santa Barbara. She wasn't that young anymore, older than your father. Then María Teresa and her parents made a big trip abroad, and there, in Europe, María Teresa married. A foreigner, if you please!" The corners of Transito's mouth dropped in disapproval. "They came back again, but María Teresa's husband couldn't stand it here. It was too quiet and remote and primitive, he said. So they went back to Europe. María Teresa died there." Transito traced the cracks in the tabletop with a black fingernail.

"Yes, the old lady has seen a lot," she added.

"I never knew that," said Carlos Arturo, who had listened breathlessly.

"No," said Transito. "You wouldn't. It's all so long ago. Your father married late. Dear Lord, I still see your mother arriving as a bride. So young, such a city girl. She never felt at home here. She never became accustomed to Payande. In the beginning I often saw her cry, poor girl." Transito's finger still slid along the cracks in the tabletop. "It must have annoyed Doña Isabel that . . . that Payande never was joined to Santa Barbara. She was used to getting her own way in everything, and she loved Santa Barbara. She was born and bred there, don't forget, and when she was a child she followed her father everywhere. Her father, Don Fausto. She adored him."

"Don Fausto?" asked Carlos Arturo. He searched his memory.

"Yes, Don Fausto. The father of Doña Isabel. The previous owner of Santa Barbara. There are not many left who knew him, but people still speak of him. He was lord and master of this region. He feared nothing, he was terribly strong, and he had a violent temper. The workers crawled for him, you may believe that! And they say that he once heaved a team of oxen into the Río Tigre, because they didn't obey him. Yes, that's what they say." Transito nodded again. "That was Don Fausto, an iron hand and an iron will."

"And that was Doña Isabel's father?" asked Carlos Arturo, half surprised, half unbelieving.

"Doña Isabel's father and owner of Santa Barbara," Transito repeated. "Yes, Don Humberto knew what he was doing when he married Doña Isabel." Transito gave an approving little nod. "But that's a long time ago. Don Fausto has been dead for years, and Don Humberto and María Teresa died within a short time of each other. May they rest in peace."

"And Doña Isabel remained alone."

"That's right, as you say, Doña Isabel survived them all: her father, her husband, and her only daughter."

And my father, thought Carlos Arturo. He stole a look at Transito. Was she going to mention him?

But Transito didn't. She got up and began to pace through the big kitchen. "She is growing very old now, the people at Santa Barbara say. Sometimes she walks in her sleep, talking to herself, they say. But then she says that somebody comes at night into the house, into the bedroom. I ask you! At night! In Santa Barbara! When Soledad, the woman who looks after her, says she locks everything up every evening." Transito heaved a deep sigh. "But that's the way it goes when you're old and have lived through so much. In the past many people visited Santa Barbara. There were always guests. Not anymore. Now she lives alone with Soledad, who looks after her. You should visit her, as I said."

Carlos Arturo did not answer. Leaning against the doorpost, he stared over the countryside. There, on the other side of the lake, behind the stone ridge, lay Santa Barbara. In that big house with the tower lived Doña Isabel, the daughter of Don Fausto, who once ruled the estate with an iron hand and who heaved a team of oxen into the Río Tigre because they did not obey him. A man who bent everyone and everything to his will.

And Doña Isabel had wanted Santa Barbara and Payande to be one estate. That was what Transito had said. Servants heard and saw more than one realized.

Silent and barefooted, they padded through the house, catching a word here, a glance there. In their own way they put things together and drew their conclusions. Instinctively they sensed the undercurrents. In the kitchens and outbuildings they discussed in whispers all they observed.

That's what they probably did after that dark and rainy night long ago, when his father disappeared. Who were the men who abducted him? Who sent them? What exactly happened? Those were the questions that occupied him constantly since he had arrived here. Why did Transito and Juan de la Cruz not answer when he brought up the subject? Why did they evade his questions? Why did people from the neighborhood not want to work on Payande? He did not know. But if he were to make Payande into a prosperous business, those questions had to be answered first.

Was his mother feeling the same way? Did she, too, think back continually to the past, to the time when his father was with them? But perhaps the situation was different for her. She had never really taken root here, as Transito had said. She did not love the land, not like Doña Isabel. Doña Isabel, who was born and brought up on Santa Barbara, who had wanted the two estates to be one. Involuntarily he thought of the Santa Barbara workers who had been cutting cane on Payande land. Perhaps Doña Isabel had sent them. Doña Isabel, who went on living on her estate after her husband and daughter had died. All alone. She must love the land very much. Enough to . . . ?

Carlos Arturo left the kitchen, his hands in his pockets, his shoulders hunched, as if he were cold. Restlessly he wandered through the halls and across the patios of the big house.

Had it been men from Santa Barbara who had come that night? He must find out . . . but how?

What if he did go to visit Doña Isabel? How would he start? What could he ask? He had no proof. Proof of what? What was it he wanted, now that he was back on Payande?

7

"Workers from Santa Barbara are cutting cane on Las Colinas," said Carlos Arturo.

"Where?" asked Doña Luisa absently.

"On Las Colinas, the hills where the sugarcane has been planted," explained Carlos Arturo a shade impatiently. His mother had lived here long enough to know the names of the different localities.

"Oh, there," said his mother. Her narrow white hand smoothed out the wrinkles in her forehead. She was tired and looked depressed. She was thinking, I knew I'd be confronted with this now that we're back again. He's a big boy now. I can't leave him in ignorance of business matters any longer. But what could I do? We needed money.

"Yes, on Las Colinas," she said wearily.

"But that's impossible," Carlos Arturo exploded

vehemently. "Las Colinas belongs to us, to Payande. What business do the workers of Santa Barbara have there? How can Doña Isabel send workers to our fields? And I have to discover this all by myself. Juan de la Cruz tells me nothing. Neither do you—" He stopped suddenly and looked at his mother, sitting there silently.

In the stillness that followed they heard noises in the back gallery—shuffling steps, wheezing, and coughing. A thin man with an unshaven face rounded the corner of the house. He remained standing and removed his frayed straw hat.

"Ah," he said slowly. "I heard that the family was here again."

Doña Luisa looked puzzled, but Carlos Arturo recognized him immediately.

"Santos," he cried.

Santos came from the mountains on the other side of the Río Tigre. There he had a piece of land, where he lived. Often in the old days he would descend on his little horse to Payande to tell Don Raúl his troubles, to unburden his heart, to ask for advice, to complain of the people who annoyed him and the things that he did not understand. There was always something. Those people from the village, they might be the mayor and the judge, were making difficulties again about the piece of land that Santos himself, with his own hands, had fenced in with barbed wire. They even came with papers he could not read. "Now I ask you, Don Raúl," he would say indignantly, "do they have to bother a poor man like me in my old age? I'll be dead soon enough!"

Or he aired his heart about that One at Santa Barbara. That One at Santa Barbara had dammed the upper course of a creek that ran through his land. Santos didn't till his land, not at all. But once it had been a pretty piece of soil, and now it was as dry as Santos's own throat.

He had sat there squatting against one of the pillars of the veranda, picking his horny toes and throwing wistful glances at the bottle of rum on the table in front of Don Raúl. Don Raúl poured a glassful and shoved it toward Santos. Contentedly sipping, Santos continued, "I always thought I might plant corn there. But what can I do with it now? Land without water is nothing. Don Raúl knows that just as well as I do." He looked at Don Raúl for confirmation, wiped his lips, and held out his glass for more.

"Who knows?" he would mutter. "This drink may be my last. I'm not what I used to be, not anymore. In the old days I could dance for two days and two nights running. All I needed was a few bottles of rum and a lot of music." His old eyes began to gleam. "My daughter has a radio, but it doesn't work. And I'm not the man I was. This year I'll die. I don't know why, but that's the way it is. One day I'll wake up dead."

Santos had any amount of time to meditate on the follies of life and what to expect at the other side of death, when that special moment came to him. He could always be found with his sons and daughters under the big mango trees in front of his hut. They would swing in hammocks in the cool shadow of the trees or sit on chairs tilted back against the broad trunks. They'd chatter for a while and gaze at the skinny chickens scratching in the dust or the bony goats that were pulling the last dried leaves from the bushes. They drank *guarapo* and beer. Their yard was a mess, and it stank in the dark house where they all slept, but they did not mind. They took life as it came. They had no thought for tomorrow. Time was all theirs; they did what they liked. They ate the bananas and yucca that grew around the house. The sons, dirty and wiry like their father, sometimes fished in the creek that flowed behind the hut. The slatternly daughters cooked and served the beer.

Sometimes one of the daughters would disappear for a while; sometimes the sons stayed away for a few nights. But they always returned to their father. Santos never worried about them, except for that time with Jacinto!

Santos had come straight to Payande to discuss it.

"The *señor* has heard already, of course, about Jacinto. It's the limit, *señor*. How can they say such things of my son! Such a good boy!"

Jacinto had been seen at the cattle fair of a neighboring village with some cows that carried the brand of La Dorada.

"It's a shame," said Santos. "I have good boys, *señor*, never had any trouble with them. That's the truth. Jacinto bought a few cows a while ago, goes to the market with them, and doesn't come back. Then I hear they've locked him up!" Santos shook his head sadly. "How is it possible! Can you tell me!"

"Well, if those cows had the brand of La Dorada . . ." began Don Raúl cautiously.

"Well, that's just it, *señor*, but Jacinto probably didn't notice. You see, the branding irons of Don Belisario and the ones we have are rather alike. . . ." And Santos, with great concentration, slowly began to trace a *B* and an *S* in the dust with his bony finger. The effort was not successful, and Santos began to sweat with exertion. At last he gave up, saying, "Anyway, why should we worry about things like that when we buy cattle just to sell again."

"Yes, but if Jacinto cannot prove that he bought them, what do you do then?"

"That's the problem, *señor*. What can an old man like me do? This year I'm sure to die, and Jacinto in prison!" For a while he stared silently in front of him, then he

68

continued, "I thought I'd better sell that piece of land after all. The *señor* has always been interested in it . . . ?" He looked questioningly at Don Raúl. "Jacinto must not stay there. That's for sure. I wasn't going to sell the land, I admit it. But now I need the money. Jacinto must not stay there. I need the money to buy him out of prison."

Carlos Arturo could not remember whether his father ever had bought Santos's patch of land. He thought of all these things as he looked at Santos, sitting with his back against a veranda pillar and picking his toes.

"So the *señora* is back," he said again. "I heard that the family was back again."

"Yes." Doña Luisa nodded. "We are back, Santos."

"For good?" asked Santos.

"That . . . that I can't say. For a while, anyway," said Doña Luisa evasively. Santos shook his head.

"So much has changed. Things are not as they were."

"No, things are not as they were," echoed Doña Luisa softly.

"And how are your sons and daughters? How is Jacinto?" Carlos Arturo asked quickly, when he saw his mother's face cloud over.

"With Jacinto?" asked Santos. "The *señor* had not heard then?"

"No, what should I have heard? What happened?"

"No one knows," said Santos dejectedly. "One evening they found him quite out of his mind. He was foaming at the mouth and was running around in circles. He yelled and moaned and cried to high heaven, laughing and weeping at the same time, saying he was afraid they would murder him. And that's how he has remained ever since, *señor*."

"What do you mean, 'that's how he has remained'?" asked Carlos Arturo.

"He just sits there and says nothing. Sometimes he starts to scream and run in circles, crying that they are going to murder him, and then there is nothing we can do with him. His head has gone wrong. That's for sure."

"How did it happen?" asked Carlos Arturo.

"We don't know, *señor*. We found him like that and so he is from one day to the other. Maybe he fell from his horse; we found it near him. But how could that be? Jacinto was a good rider, a very good rider. He was a good boy too, always kind to his old father. I'm not young anymore. This year I'll die. I feel it." Santos got up. He took leave of Doña Luisa and shuffled over the wide veranda to the back steps where his horse stood.

Carlos Arturo went with him. I didn't offer him a glass of rum, he suddenly thought, as my father would have done. Aloud he said, "I'm sorry to hear about Jacinto. It's very strange."

"Yes, *señor*, but strange things do happen."

Yes, thought Carlos Arturo, the way something strange happened to my father. His father had disappeared overnight. Men had come in the darkness. One of them on a white horse.

"Santos," he said suddenly, "who has a white horse around here?"

"A white horse?" asked Santos. "A white horse? Why? Do you want to buy one?"

"No, I was just curious," Carlos Arturo said evasively. Santos stared at him.

"A white horse . . ." he said slowly. "Don Belisario rides a white horse."

8

Branches reached out to the jeep, hooking into the canvas top. Everything was neglected and decayed, thought Carlos Arturo sadly. Weeds almost obliterated the path to the road, the flowering shrubs demanded more and more space, one of the entrance pillars had been damaged, and the iron gates were unhinged.

The jeep bounced along the narrow country road as he drove in the direction of La Dorada.

He had been debating the whole afternoon whether he would go. Finally he got into the jeep and now was on his way to see Don Belisario.

He had no idea what he was going to say or do there. The thing was to find out whether Don Belisario had indeed a white horse. If that were so, what would it prove? A white horse . . . a white horse . . . that he had caught a glimpse of long ago on a rainy night.

White hindquarters, quickly turning away, in the rain, in the dark. A glimmer, nothing more.

At first, when Carlos Arturo had lived at his grandmother's in the city, he had expected his father to come soon and fetch him, to bring his mother and himself back to Payande. When he came home from school in the afternoon, he always hoped to see his father in the living room, chatting with his mother and grandmother. Later, in bed, he imagined he heard the familiar step in the hall, on the stairs. He would gaze at the door of his room in the darkness till his eyes ached. But the door did not open.

Instead, when he came home from school, his grandmother usually was sitting in the little antechamber with some embroidery and his mother was upstairs in the bedroom lying down with a headache, the drapes drawn.

The living room would be empty.

Slowly the memories of his father faded. Finally he seldom thought of him. But now he was back on Payande, and the past was coming alive again, preoccupying him each day anew. He wanted to know!

Perhaps Don Belisario . . . he would chat with him about the cattle, ask his advice, and gradually, casually bring up old times.

The jeep bounced over the road in a cloud of dust. Iguanas that had been basking in the middle of the road in the late sun darted off. To the left was the bar, Las Delicias, and to the right began the high dirt wall, overgrown with cactus plants. Between tall bushes he saw the entrance of La Dorada. Carlos Arturo stopped the car and walked to the gate to push it open. But it was locked with a thick iron chain and a rusty padlock. The gate rattled when he shook it, but it remained shut.

"Rosalina has the key."

"What?"

"Rosalina has the key, if you want it." The girl stood in the middle of the road in a tight, faded red dress. Her brown legs were muscular, and the toes of her bare feet moved in the dust. Untidy curls hung over her shoulders. She brushed away a strand of hair and laughed. Her eyes had a pert gleam, her lips were full, and her teeth white and savage.

"Are you going to see Don Belisario?"

"Yes."

"You're from Payande, aren't you?"

"Yes."

"Rosalina has the key. You have to get it there."

"Where? Who is Rosalina?"

"Edelio's Rosalina. You know, Edelio who had the accident. Rosalina has the key. You can get it there."

"And where does Rosalina live?"

"Nearby on the other side of the bridge. You can

walk it. But I don't know if she's home. She had to go to Ana-Amanda. One of the kids is sick again." She shrugged her shoulders. "Rosalina's children are always sick. Rosalina keeps going back and forth to Ana-Amanda. Before Edelio used to go, but now he is dead. . . ." She shrugged again.

"The accident was here at the bridge, wasn't it?" Carlos Arturo involuntarily glanced at the bridge, a little farther on by the bend in the road.

"People say he was drunk, but that isn't true."

"How do you know?"

"Because he hadn't been at our place that evening. We saw him pass in the Santa Barbara pickup. He drove as if the devil was after him, and he didn't stop the way he usually did. He went straight on."

"What do you mean 'our place'? Who are you?"

"Don't you know me? I am Blanca of Las Delicias, and Edelio wasn't in our place that evening."

"Where did you say Rosalina lives?"

"On the other side of the bridge. To the left. You'll see it right away."

Carlos Arturo thanked her and got into the jeep again.

"Watch out at the bridge!" Blanca called after him and laughed.

Pale, dirty children played around the hut. Rosalina wasn't there, but the oldest girl gave him the key.

When he returned to the gate of La Dorada, Blanca had vanished.

Carlos Arturo opened the gate, drove through, and shut the gate behind him. La Dorada was green and hilly. Here and there palms grew, and cattle grazed everywhere. Beautiful, fat, shiny cattle. A narrow track curved through the pasture. There were many fences that separated the different herds of cattle and many improvised gates of barbed wire. Carlos Arturo had to keep stopping and getting out to open and close them. The track seemed endless. It was already growing dark in the valleys among the palms. He saw no houses anywhere. The road came to an end at a sluggish little river. Carlos Arturo hesitated for a moment. On the other side he seemed to see cart tracks faintly showing in the grass. Taking a chance, he splashed across the stream and again followed a track that now was no more than a rut in the high grass. He had difficulty making it out in the fading light and began to wonder if he was going in the right direction. Perhaps he had passed Don Belisario's house, or perhaps it didn't exist.

But it must exist. He remembered a large house where he used to play . . . play with whom? He couldn't remember. His mother hadn't commented when he had talked about La Dorada that first evening when they arrived. And Juan de la Cruz had talked of other things. "The cattle are good on La Dorada."

That's what Juan de la Cruz had said. It was true too. The cattle, shadowy now in the twilight, looked healthy. Better than the cattle on Payande.

It was now almost completely dark, but after rounding a bend in the track he suddenly saw light. A large house loomed. Through the tall windows light streamed out. Dogs began to bark and surrounded the jeep. Before Carlos Arturo could get out, the door opened and a big, heavy man stood in the doorway of the house.

"Quiet," he told the dogs, looking at the jeep. He stood there unmoving, large, broadshouldered, with a paunch that heaved over his khaki trousers.

"The jeep from Payande . . ." he said slowly. "Well, well."

Carlos Arturo introduced himself. "We have come back again," he continued. "And now I . . . I thought . . . came. . . ." he blundered into silence.

"And now you come to visit me," Don Belisario said softly. Then he added more softly, as if he spoke to himself, "You have a nerve."

He turned and went inside. Carlos Arturo followed him. They entered an enormous room. The walls were white and very high. Two fluorescent lights on the ceiling lighted the room to its farthest corners with a cold blue radiance. There was only one piece of furniture.

Don Belisario turned and looked searchingly at Carlos Arturo. His face was set grimly. One of his eyes was white and watery and had no pupil.

"So you came back anyway," said Don Belisario.

"Yes, we are back," said Carlos Arturo. He felt uncomfortable under the penetrating stare of that one eye.

"Do you play billiards?"

"What? What did you say?" stammered Carlos Arturo.

Don Belisario walked to the one piece of furniture in the center of the room. He reached out and stroked the billiard table.

"I asked, do you play billiards?"

"Sometimes, a little," answered Carlos Arturo, bewildered.

"Let's see what you can do," ordered Don Belisario. He offered Carlos Arturo a cue and pointed to the balls on the green baize. Nervously Carlos Arturo bent over. He let the cue slip through his fingers. He aimed at the yellowed ivory ball and hit it. The ball rolled over the baize, reached a second, struck the edge of the table, rolled back, and knocked at a third. When the balls stopped moving they were far apart. Carlos Arturo looked at them. He felt Don Belisario's one eye on him as he walked slowly around the table and bent over again. The eye followed all his movements.

Again the cue glided through his fingers and hit the ball, shooting it over the green baize till it came to a halt in the farthest corner.

Don Belisario come slowly to life. Gingerly he walked around the table with his cue, his eye on the balls. He bent his huge body. *Click, click, click, click, click* . . . the balls knocked together monotonously, regularly. They congregated in a corner of the table. *Click, click, click, click.* His one eye was on the baize, on the ivory balls. He seemed to have forgotten Carlos Arturo.

At the back of the room a door opened. A servant appeared with a glass of fruit juice on a saucer. She shuffled to the staircase at the opposite end of the room.

Click. The ball dawdled and came to a stop. Don Belisario straightened up. He looked at the maid with the fruit juice and then at Carlos Arturo.

"Put that glass of juice in the dining room," he ordered. "And bring me the *aguardiente*." He put the cue in the rack and led Carlos Arturo between tall pillars to the dining room at the back. The maid crept after them with the fruit juice.

They sat down at the table. The maid put the juice in front of Carlos Arturo and disappeared. She came back a moment later with a bottle of *aguardiente* and a glass.

They drank silently, facing each other across the

79

table. Carlos Arturo saw the maid, with another glass of fruit juice, go through the hall toward the staircase. The steps creaked. Upstairs a door slammed. Don Belisario drank greedily. He poured himself another glass, spilling some of the brandy on the tablecloth. He drank it in one draft and filled his glass again, spilling some more.

"Why did you come back?" he asked.

"Because of Payande. The land has been badly neglected."

"No wonder when no one has cared for it."

"Juan de la Cruz did his best, but he is old."

"It's a miracle that he stayed at all."

"He worked for so long on Payande. He worked for my grandfather and my father."

"Juan de la Cruz is an old fool," Don Belisario broke in rudely. His one eye stared malevolently at Carlos Arturo. Then he continued, "He thought he could have his way, here in the valley. He thought he could do as he pleased. Proud and obstinate, that he was. . . . Ah, but there were still people who stood up to him." Again he emptied his glass in one draft. The *aguardiente* dribbled down on his chin. He re-filled his glass at once and spilled some more.

Carlos Arturo fidgeted in his chair. He wanted to get away. He felt ill at ease in that huge, quiet house, in that half-lighted room with the old man, who kept drinking and staring at him with his one eye.

"Do you see that?" said Don Belisario. He pointed to his bad eye. "I can thank him for that. If only that had been all!" He spilled more *aguardiente* as he brought his glass to his lips. It ran down his chin. He paid no attention to it.

"If I were you I would take care to leave Payande as soon as possible. That place is bankrupt." His voice was getting thicker. "Though the mills of God grind slowly, yet they grind exceeding small. Don't forget that. Exceeding small."

"But . . . but what in the world can Juan de la Cruz have done?" asked Carlos Arturo hesitantly.

There was a moment of quiet. Don Belisario stared at him, astonished, half unbelieving. "What did you say?" He felt again for the bottle. "Juan de la Cruz? You don't mean to tell me that you don't *know?* That you don't understand what I'm talking about?" He slipped farther down into his chair, with the bottle in one hand and the glass in the other, and suddenly burst into loud, uncontrolled laughter.

It sounded gloomily hollow in that silent house, echoing into the room with the billiard table. Carlos Arturo sprang up. Suddenly he did not want to know what Don Belisario was talking about. He wanted to get away, away from this house and the bare room and this old, half-drunken man with his white eye and wet chin and hysterical laughter.

"I have to go," he yelled through the noise of

81

laughter. Silence descended, but the one eye kept looking at him.

"Yes, go, and leave Payande to its fate," said the old man thickly. He still sat there with his glass and his bottle.

Upstairs a door creaked. There were muffled voices. The maid came down the staircase. She cast a timid look toward the dining room as she crept through the big room.

Carlos Arturo walked quickly after her. She disappeared into the kitchen as he pulled open the front door.

A man stood on the steps. He let Carlos Arturo pass and called from the doorway, "Can I do anything more for you, Don Belisario?"

"No, no. You can go. I don't need you anymore. I need no one. Put my horse away. That's all."

"Yes, *mi patrón*. At your service, *mi patrón*. Good night, *mi patrón*." The man pulled the door shut and vanished into the darkness.

Carlos Arturo forced himself to step calmly into the jeep and start the motor. He moved slowly, but he knew he was taking flight. Carefully he turned the car. In the light of the headlights he saw the farmhand sending a horse into the meadow with a slap on the flank.

It was a large white horse.

9

Blanca sat alone in the dim interior of the bar with the bottles and the glass cases of candies. A candle burned on the counter. She saw the jeep stop, and when Carlos Arturo entered, her eyes gleamed.

"A lemonade, please," said Carlos Arturo casually.

Blanca opened the bottle deftly on a crooked nail and slid it across the sticky counter. She bent over, her firm brown arms resting on the wooden top. The candlelight shone on her broad face with its high cheekbones and full lips.

"Did you get there?" she asked.

"Where?" asked Carlos Arturo evasively. He didn't quite know why he had dropped into Las Delicias.

"Didn't you go to La Dorada?"

"Yes. So what?"

"Did you see her?"

"Who?" asked Carlos Arturo. "What are you talking about?"

Blanca looked at him with glowing eyes. "I suppose you want me to think you don't know," she mocked. "Yet you've been to La Dorada. Didn't I tell you Rosalina had the key?"

"One of the children gave it to me. Rosalina wasn't home."

"That's what I thought. I saw her go this afternoon. I know where she went. To Ana-Amanda." She looked triumphant.

"Yes," said Carlos Arturo. "That's what you told me."

"Everyone goes to Ana-Amanda," said Blanca. "She can cure anything. She knows a lot about sickness and has medicine for everything. She makes it herself. Everyone who is sick goes to her. And at Rosalina's they are always sick."

Carlos Arturo raised an eyebrow. "Then Ana-Amanda isn't such a miracle doctor as people think," he said scornfully. The laughter suddenly went out of Blanca's eyes. She looked furtively around the dim bar.

"Watch out," she warned. "Watch out what you're saying! If Ana-Amanda should hear you! And she finds out everything. She *knows* everything, and they say she has ways of looking into the future."

"Who says that?" asked Carlos Arturo, but his voice was no longer scornful. He had been frightened by Blanca's reaction.

"Oh, the people here around the lake. I often hear them. I hear a lot." Blanca's fingertip, red with chipped red nail polish, made designs on the counter. "Perhaps Rosalina went to Ana-Amanda to find out exactly what happened to Edelio." From under her tangled hair she looked slyly at Carlos Arturo.

"But Edelio had an accident at the bridge," said Carlos Arturo. He shifted his weight from one leg to the other. He suddenly felt ill at ease.

"Yes, at the bridge . . . there was an accident there before."

Carlos Arturo did not say anything. He twisted the sticky lemonade bottle between his hands.

"Did Don Belisario mention it to you?"

"To me? No. Why?"

Again Blanca gave him a sly look, as if they both knew something that was better left unsaid, as if they shared a secret.

"No reason. I just asked. Do you want anything else? A glass of beer?"

"No, thanks."

"I'll hide the bottle under the counter, so you won't have to pay. No one will know."

"No. No, thanks." Carlos Arturo got ready to go.

"That's sixty centavos," Blanca said smartly.

"Oh, yes, of course." He blushed and hastened to put the money for the lemonade on the counter. The stubby brown hand with the chipped red nails slid the money from the counter into the pocket of the tight red dress.

"I still don't understand why Rosalina had to go to Ana-Amanda to find out something about Edelio's accident," said Carlos Arturo, who could not resist reopening the subject. "You say Ana-Amanda can see the future."

"The future or the past, it's all the same," Blanca answered placidly. "Ana-Amanda knows everything. She even sees things that aren't there."

"What do you mean, 'things that aren't there'?"

Blanca shrugged her shoulders impatiently. "Gone. Lost."

Carlos Arturo stared at her.

"My mother has had the experience herself," Blanca continued. "She went to Ana-Amanda once when she lost her scissors and Ana-Amanda asked her to come back again by a waning moon. So my mother did, and Ana-Amanda told her exactly where the scissors were. And sure enough, my mother found them, under a bag of cornmeal." Blanca looked triumphantly at Carlos Arturo. "And then there was the lost cow from Santa Barbara. They went to Ana-Amanda, and Ana-

Amanda said she saw the cow up in the mountains above the Río Tigre, where Santos lives."

"And?" asked Carlos Arturo, when Blanca fell silent.

"That's all. They found her there," answered Blanca.

"Perhaps Jacinto led her there," suggested Carlos Arturo.

"Ah, Jacinto," said Blanca slowly. "Isn't that something! He's no good for anything anymore, poor fellow. He's not even fit to steal cattle. They say he's completely off his head. He gets fits and . . . hallicinatics."

"Hallucinations," corrected Carlos Arturo mechanically.

"That's it." Blanca laughed. Her white teeth glistened. "Everyone has some trouble." Deftly she opened two bottles of beer and shoved one over the counter at Carlos Arturo. "Here," she said. "You get a dry throat from all that talking."

"That's true," said Carlos Arturo. They drank the beer.

"Did your mother say anything else? About Ana-Amanda, I mean? How is it that she can know where lost things are and the past and so on?"

Blanca shrugged her shoulders impatiently. "I've told you already. Ana-Amanda just sat there, staring through my mother as if she wasn't there. My mother told her about the scissors and asked where she could have put them, and then Ana-Amanda began to talk and explained exactly where she could find them."

"But how does Ana-Amanda know?" asked Carlos Arturo.

Blanca threw him a pitying smile. "As if she'd tell her secrets to anyone," she said. "Everything she knows she learned from her mother. Her mother came from far away, from behind the mountains. She was a cook in one of the big houses around here." She fell silent and scrutinized Carlos Arturo through half-closed eyes. "Don't tell me that you don't know that either."

Carlos Arturo didn't answer directly. "I've been away for so long, and I don't like gossip."

"Oh, no?" Blanca asked teasingly. She leaned far over the counter and made a challenging motion with her head. Her tangled jet-black hair fell forward. The candle flickered. He smelled the scent of her skin.

Suddenly he noticed how close it was in the small, half-dark bar. Quickly he laid four pesos on the counter, but Blanca's finger with the red nail shoved the bills back to him.

"Till the next time," she said with a little smile.

"Yes . . . er . . . yes," stammered Carlos Arturo.

With a rush he started off in the old jeep. It was dark, but here and there a light twinkled. He met a few men on horseback. Were they on their way to Las Delicias? It was probably true that Blanca heard a lot. Stories about Ana-Amanda, who could see into the future—and the past. Stories about Santa Barbara, La Dorada, and, of course, Payande.

What had she meant when she asked, "Did you see her?" Who was he supposed to have seen at La Dorada? Don Belisario, the lonely, grudging man with his one eye? The timid maid climbing the stairs? He only had heard the creaking door, the whispering voices.

Who sat there, upstairs in that great, locked-up house? In that house where only a billiard table stood in the middle of the main room?

"Did you see her?" Blanca had said. He heard the words plainly. And Blanca wouldn't have made a mistake. Blanca wasn't someone who made mistakes easily. She heard all the stories of the neighborhood. She knew everything. Blanca with the tangled hair, her impish laugh, and the gleaming teeth of a wildcat. Blanca, bold and challenging.

He entered the gate of Payande. For the first time since he had come back he wasn't thinking of his father.

10

He couldn't get to sleep. With eyes wide open he gazed into the darkness. Outside the silence was broken by the croaking of frogs and the monotonous chant of crickets. A branch moved in front of the open window. It was hot.

Carlos Arturo tossed restlessly. That one eye of Don Belisario, that white eye without a pupil, seemed to stare at him out of the darkness. He wished he hadn't gone to visit La Dorada. That horrible, remote house. The big room with the billiard table. And Don Belisario, half slumped in his chair in the dining room with his bottle of *aguardiente* and his wet chin. The nonsense he had babbled about Juan de la Cruz's thinking he could have his own way and doing as he liked, being proud and obstinate!

But that description did not fit Juan de la Cruz. He

must have been talking about someone else. About whom then?

"You don't mean to tell me that you don't know," Don Belisario had said. And Blanca. She had used almost the same words. Both had laughed, in a different way. The hysterical laughter of Don Belisario had frightened him. It still rang in his ears. What was it he did not know? Whom had Don Belisario spoken about so bitterly? His father? What had happened between those two? Had Don Belisario been one of the men who had come that night, the leader, perhaps? He had a white horse and a white eye. A white eye that kept staring at him out of the darkness.

Carlos Arturo wiped the sweat from his forehead. Getting up, he went to the window. It was cooler there. The sky was alight with stars. In the distance he could make out a dark ring of trees. The trees that edged the lake.

They often had gone fishing there, his father and he. For hours they had sat in the little rowboat with a fishing rod, gazing over the water. He remembered the lilac shine of the water hyacinths, water birds tripping over the leaves with quick, fine legs, white herons silhouetted against dense foliage, the quiet of the lake. Sometimes the silence was broken by a snapping twig and the rustling tread of someone passing on the shore.

"Somebody's going to Ana-Amanda," Carlos Arturo would remark. His father would frown. "Poor soul," he would say, irritated.

"But if someone is ill. . . ." Carlos Arturo ventured. When his father did not answer, he added, "Everyone says that Ana-Amanda knows everything about healing herbs."

"Yes," said Don Raúl. "You can't blame them really. They don't know any better. For centuries they've consulted medicine men or women like Ana-Amanda, people whom they fear but from whom they can't free themselves. If you try to help them in your own way with modern medicine, they become suspicious and confused and even more frustrated than they are already. It's hard, but it will have to end sometime. People like Ana-Amanda do a lot of harm."

"But she does help everyone, and she is very wise," Carlos Arturo couldn't resist saying. He thought of Transito and Juan de la Cruz, and all the other people around who spoke with awe of Ana-Amanda.

"She helps everyone, even when she cannot help, in order not to lose her prestige. Take what happened to El Cojo, for instance."

Carlos Arturo remembered that incident very well. El Cojo was an old man who lived alone in his hut in the mountains. He always had worked on Santa Barbara until his foot got caught in the wheel of the sugar mill. The accident caused a sensation in the valley. For miles around people heard him yell. Everyone came running, and Ana-Amanda was fetched immediately.

The mangled foot looked horrible. Ana-Amanda treated it with snake's fat and the dried leaves of the Santa María. She immediately poured one of her strange brews between the lips of El Cojo, who at that time still was known by the name of Juan Manuel. The potion silenced him and made him sleep. Carlos Arturo witnessed the whole thing from beginning to end. His parents had gone to the city to visit his grandmother, so he ran along with the others to the sugar mill to see what had happened.

When his parents came back, he told them the whole story, full of excitement, and Carlos Arturo could remember very clearly his father's grim face. Don Raúl went at once to visit El Cojo and found him in his hut. El Cojo's foot was one stinking wound and the leg purple and swollen. They brought him to Payande on a stretcher and from there immediately to the doctor in the village and as soon as possible to the hospital in the city. Juan Manuel was away a long time, and when he came back he had only one leg. The whole valley buzzed with the news, and since then everyone called him El Cojo, the lame one.

El Cojo didn't mind. He said that the lost leg was

one worry less, but he would not go back to Santa Barbara. From that day he wandered through the mountains on his little horse. Sometimes he washed gold in the rivers. Sometimes he searched for the treasures that the Indians had buried along with their chiefs. So he lived. Once in a while he came to Payande to show what he had found. Then he and Don Raúl sat together on the back steps. Between them was a dirty pouch full of strange articles. Carlos Arturo remembered that pouch very well. El Cojo had made it himself out of string.

The last time he came visiting he had suddenly said: "When is the *señor* going?"

"Going?" Don Raúl had asked. "What do you mean?"

"Ah. I thought the *señor* would be going. Going away from Payande."

"Away from Payande! What gave you that idea?"

"Well, what shall I say . . . ? You hear a thing or two when you're wandering around like me. The *señor* should go." Slowly he packed his things.

"The very idea! To go away just when the rainy season is starting. You know better than that, Juan Manuel." His father never called El Cojo by his nickname.

"Yes, *señor*, the rainy season starts soon. Before the rainy season, that would be best. . . ." And with these enigmatic words El Cojo vanished into the darkness.

Not long afterward, on a night when the rain fell in torrents, when the waters of the Río Tigre foamed and the rocks moaned in its stony bed. . . . A night when he had stood at the window just as he was standing now.

What, thought Carlos Arturo, had El Cojo known? For he had known something. In his own queer way he wanted to warn Don Raúl. Why didn't he make the warning plainer? Why didn't he say right out what he had heard or guessed? But it was not in the nature of these country people to speak plainly. They were always devious, especially when ill at ease or afraid.

Afraid!

Of whom had El Cojo been afraid? If only he could find out! He gazed over the land, lying so peacefully under the starry sky, the dark hills and mountains in the distance. There, hidden in the rolling hills, stood the big country houses, La Dorada and Santa Barbara. There in the mountains lived El Cojo. Why shouldn't he go and visit El Cojo?

11

Carlos Arturo had gone with Sabas to look at the cattle. The young animals had been branded with the irons of Payande and had been numbered. In the evenings Carlos Arturo spent a lot of time bent over the books in his father's study doing paper work.

"The different plots must be fenced in, Sabas."

"Yes, *señor*."

"When do you think you can start on the job?"

"Who knows, *señor*?"

"The sooner the better, I think."

"Yes, *señor*."

"Sometime next week then."

"Yes, *señor*, but there is no barbed wire."

"I'll bring you some when we go to the village."

"Yes, *señor*. There are no posts either."

Carlos Arturo repressed a sigh. "We used to hew

them out of the quarry farther up in the mountains. We could go and look at it and send some men there."

"Yes, *señor*."

"As soon as possible then." They had had a similar conversation before, he remembered with a discouraged sigh. Then he recollected that El Cojo's hut was not far from the quarry.

"How is El Cojo?" he asked.

Sabas stared at him.

"El Cojo," repeated Carlos Arturo. "Who lives up there."

"Yes, *señor*," said Sabas.

Carlos Arturo didn't bother to ask again. They rode together for a while longer, then they separated, and each went his way. Communication with these people was difficult, thought Carlos Arturo. They could talk only about the cattle. Sabas knew all about them. He was one of the best cowhands in the whole district. It would be a pity if he left, but Carlos knew that he could not keep him if Sabas really wanted to leave. So far Sabas had said nothing about his plan. Only Carmencita had blurted it out. And Carlos Arturo was wise enough not to bring up the subject himself. The longer Sabas stayed, the better it was for him. But he was worried. Perhaps, he thought, they are waiting till Carmencita has her baby. Then he would not have much time to find a substitute. And where would he find a good reliable one? He couldn't take just any-body. A head *vaquero* was a trusted person, someone to depend on, who knew a lot about cattle. Like Sabas.

Replacing him wouldn't be easy.

He could inquire tentatively in the village. They would have to go there soon anyway. He felt a distaste for the village after he and his mother had stood there like strangers when they first arrived.

Perhaps Santos could give him advice. Santos had lived so long in the region that he knew everybody. He had come so often with his problems to Payande that his giving advice for once was only fair. And if Santos by chance knew someone suitable, perhaps he then would exert his influence so that the person would work on Payande, which was another problem.

He turned his horse and rode up the mountains through long dry grass, dense shrubbery, and narrow creeks with white, foaming water.

Carlos Arturo found Santos in his hammock under the mango trees. He was surrounded by empty beer bottles and bits of refuse. Chickens, goats, and pigs all rooted around. A few slovenly young women peered around the corner of the hut when the dogs started to bark.

Santos scrambled up out of his hammock, and Carlos Arturo dismounted.

"Well, there we have Don Carlos Arturo. How are

you! What good fortune to see you!" Then, to his daughters, "Bring beer for Don Carlos Arturo from Payande." And then again to Carlos Arturo, "You'll have some, won't you? It's not every day we get visitors."

"Yes," said Carlos Arturo, nodding. "If it's not too much trouble. I'd love a drink. It's hot today, and I've been out all morning looking at the cattle."

"Ah," said Santos. "The cattle. Yes, it's hot today. Very hot. I've never known it to be so hot." Turning to his daughters, he shouted, "Bring a chair for Don Carlos Arturo, and the beer, do you hear?"

They brought the beer and the chair, then quickly withdrew to the safety of the hut and the smoky little kitchen.

Carlos Arturo and Santos sat side by side in the shadow of the mango trees, Santos rocking contentedly on the edge of his hammock. They drank the beer.

"So you were looking at the cattle," said Santos.

"Yes, I want to put up new fences between the grazing grounds the way Don Belisario has them."

"Who?" asked Santos.

"Don Belisario. I've been there recently, and the cattle looked fat and gleaming."

"So you were there, at Don Belisario's. At Don Belisario's," repeated Santos. "Well, well."

"Why do you say that?" asked Carlos Arturo

quickly. "Why do you think it strange that I went there? Aren't we neighbors? La Dorada and Payande share a common boundary."

Santos nodded. "Very true," he said, "and it has caused a lot of trouble."

"Trouble about what?"

Santos did not answer immediately. He rolled the beer bottle between his dirty, bony fingers. "Trouble, always trouble about water, of course. What else? What else would one have trouble about besides water? If you can't irrigate your land . . . and Don Raúl, your father, was not an easy man. One had to be friends with him, I can tell you. He had a temper, a terrible temper, and when it was up, there was nothing one could do with him. Like the time. . . ." Santos stroked his wrinkled face. "Ah, that was something."

Carlos Arturo sat very still. "Go on," he said, when Santos stayed silent.

"It's a long time ago, but it's the kind of thing you don't forget. Don Belisario wanted to dam one of his little rivers to make a reservoir of water for the dry season. Don Raúl knew of it, of course. They often had exchanged words over it. For if Don Belisario did that, then part of Payande would be without water. One afternoon Don Raúl passed in a jeep and saw the workers of La Dorada busy building a dam in the river. Well, he was furious. And when Don Raúl got really mad, a person had to watch out, like I said. He stopped and got out, went to the workers, and drew his revolver. He said if they didn't stop working immediately, he'd shoot the lot of them, including their *patrón*, who wasn't there, of course."

"Shoot them?" asked Carlos Arturo.

"Yes." Santos nodded. "And he would have done it too," he added with a certain amount of satisfaction.

"But he couldn't do a thing like that!" said Carlos Arturo.

"Well," said Santos tolerantly, "you have to defend your rights with your right hand. What else can a man do?" When Carlos Arturo didn't reply, he added, "A hacienda without water is nothing. I've had my own troubles on that score with that One from Santa Barbara. But what can you expect? I'm an old man, and I'm going to die this year. Why, I don't know."

"And then . . . what happened then?" asked Carlos Arturo. His thoughts were filled with his father and the workers who were damming up the river. He saw them standing up to their hips in the water, the revolver pointing at them. "What happened then?" he asked.

"What happened? Well, nothing! Except for the accident, of course. Don Belisario heard about the row with Don Raúl even before he got back to La Dorada from a visit to the village. He was furious that Don

Raúl had dared to interfere with his plans and had threatened him as well. He swore that he would get even with him once and for all. I think he meant to go straight to Payande, but before he could get there the accident happened at the bridge."

"An accident at the bridge?"

"Yes, the boy was killed at once. People say that Don Belisario in his anger turned too abruptly. The car fell off the bridge into the river. That's the way it happened, and the boy was killed immediately, like I said."

"Which boy?"

"Which boy? His son, of course. Don Belisario's son. Don Belisario is married to the notary's sister, as you know. When Don Belisario went to the village, he'd take the little boy with him to play at his uncle's house. And that afternoon as he and the boy were driving back Don Belisario heard about Don Raúl and the dam, and that's when the accident happened."

Santos slowly poured the rest of the beer down his throat. He smacked his lips. "Yes, it's a long time ago, a very long time ago. I'm getting old. Someday I'll wake up dead. I don't know why."

Carlos Arturo stared into the distance. His father chasing the workers of La Dorada from a dam in the river with a revolver. Don Belisario driving into the Río Tigre in a fit of temper. . . . The son of Don

Belisario was the boy he had played with. Carlos Arturo knew now that he had played with that boy, not much older than himself, at La Dorada.

He said slowly, "I saw Blanca a while ago. She knew I had come from Don Belisario, and she asked if I had seen some woman. She acted very mysterious and looked at me as if I knew what she meant. But I didn't know what she was talking about."

Santos stared at the empty beer bottle. "Blanca?" he repeated. "Blanca?"

"Yes, Blanca of Las Delicias."

"Ah, Blanca." Santos began to cackle with laughter. His old face dissolved into wrinkles, his little eyes glistened. "Ah, Blanca. You talked to her? You'd better watch your step!"

"Why?"

"Blanca is a bad one," old Santos said, savoring each word. He turned to the untidy women near the hut and called for more beer. But Carlos Arturo said he did not want any more. He rose hastily. There was so much to think about. He had forgotten completely the reason why he had gone to Santos in the first place. He picked up the empty beer bottles absentmindedly and walked with them to the hut.

Inside, in the half dark, he saw a man lying in a hammock, his feet dangling over the side. With an empty, expressionless gaze he stared at Carlos Arturo, standing in the doorway. It was a moment before Carlos Arturo realized who he was.

"Jacinto," he said.

"Eh . . ." said Jacinto. He did not move. No spark of recognition lighted his staring eyes.

"I'm Carlos Arturo, of Payande. . . ."

One of the young women hastily left the smoky little kitchen. "Let him alone," she said. "He doesn't understand anything. He lives in another world. Now he's quiet, but when he has a fit we have to tie him up."

"Eh . . ." said Jacinto. His face was yellow and sunken, his eyes wide open, and he kept swallowing as if his throat were dry. A little ashamed, Carlos Arturo retreated. It was terrible to meet such a human wreck, dirty, apathetic, and totally isolated. He took leave quickly and rode off through the gate.

The young women peered after him. They whispered and giggled as they brought their father the extra beer he had asked for.

Santos sank back in his hammock where he swung contentedly in the shade of the trees. "Ah," he muttered, "I've seen a thing or two. I'm old. This year I'll surely die. I don't know why."

12

"What else," said his mother, "could I have done?"

Carlos Arturo did not answer. He felt defeated. The truth, which he now knew, was harder to bear than he had expected. For, of course, he had had his suspicions. "But," he said gently, "our land . . . it was our land, Payande's land."

"You'll have to look at it differently," coaxed his mother. "Every year we got less from the hacienda. The workers had to be paid, and the debt to the bank. And we could not let my family pay for everything. Your grandmother had always been very kind to us. But the school fees had to be paid, and our clothes. As it was, Uncle Ernesto felt that we were staying with my mother too long. He thought the two of us were too much for her."

"Uncle Ernesto," said Carlos Arturo bitterly. "What

did he care for Payande? When he visited us in the old days, he only came to hunt and fish and play the country gentleman."

"Shame on you, Carlos Arturo," his mother told him. "I don't want to hear you talk that way. Uncle Ernesto helped us with everything since we . . . since our lives changed suddenly."

"Yes," Carlos Arturo interrupted her coldly. "He helped us to sell our land, our own land, which he had no right to do."

"He did have the right," his mother said reproachfully. "He had a power of attorney."

"A power of attorney?"

"Yes, we found it in your father's desk in his study."

"Did you know about it?"

"I? No . . . but I knew so little of your father's affairs. He never told me anything." She sat with her hands clenched together, her eyes on the tablecloth. He suddenly pitied her. She must have had a difficult time. The horrible insecurity of those first years after his father's death, living on memories in her mother's house, owning a country estate that, instead of providing her with money, swallowed it all up.

Carlos Arturo was beginning to understand the problem since they had returned. There was always something that had to be bought or replaced or repaired. There were always more expenses. Payande was no less beloved, no less fascinating, but no longer was it the paradise of his childhood.

His mother had risen. He heard her footsteps recede and the closing of the door of her room.

Carlos Arturo got up, too, and went to his father's study. A lot of work lay waiting for him, but he sat idle and listless in front of the desk. Night was falling, but he did not call Transito to bring him a lamp.

This was the truth then. For years Payande had been sold piece by piece to Santa Barbara. That's why Santa Barbara's men had cut the sugarcane of Las Colinas. His Uncle Ernesto had used his father's power of attorney to sell the land. He had misused shamefully the trust his father had placed in him. For Carlos Arturo knew with certainty that his father never had meant to sell that land. Why had his father given a power of attorney to Uncle Ernesto?

Or had he? His mother had said that they found the power of attorney in the desk, though she never knew it existed. His father and Uncle Ernesto never had been intimate. Uncle Ernesto was, like his mother, a city person. Life in the country hadn't interested him, and he had seldom come to Payande. Yet, after his father disappeared, they had found a power of attorney, and then piece by piece they had sold the land to Santa Barbara. Santa Barbara were Doña Isabel lived.

But Doña Isabel had known his father well. She had

107

known that he loved his land. She must have realized that he never would have wanted to sell it, even though there was a power of attorney. Or had she foreseen that when the owner of Payande disappeared, these things would happen? Had she then been able to fulfill her dearest wish: to have Santa Barbara and Payande come under one management? He still heard Transito telling him about her. The room became darker. The heavy furniture and the big bookcase with its moldy books became vague shadows. A moist wind blew over the meadows and brought a scent from long ago. . . .

His father, large, strong, sunburned, energetic, and self-assured. His loud voice echoing through the house. Always gay, always ready to make plans. Fishing in the lake, swimming in the river, endless journeys on horseback over the hacienda. Together they had visited people in the small huts around the lake. His father knew them all. He knew about their worries and was always ready to help. That is how Carlos Arturo remembered his father. But his mother had said, "He never told me anything." And Don Belisario, staring at him with his one good eye, had called him proud. "Someone who thought he could do as he pleased."

What, thought Carlos Arturo dejectedly, did he really know about his father?

A man with a revolver in his hand, standing on the

edge of the river where the men of La Dorada were building a dam and threatening to shoot them. A man who defended his rights with his right hand as Santos had said approvingly. That was his father too.

And now there was no one to defend the rights of Payande. Its cattle looked scrawny, and Santa Barbara's men harvested the sugarcane on Las Colinas.

Doña Isabel once had hoped that her daughter would marry Don Raúl from Payande, but his father had gone to the city. He had forgotten the girl he had played with as a child. Finally he had come home with his young city bride.

By then María Teresa, Doña Isabel's daughter, was living abroad, married to a foreigner. Doña Isabel was left behind, alone . . . an embittered woman perhaps. Bitter enough to. . . .

Carlos Arturo rose. He began to pace the floor. But how could Doña Isabel have known that there was a power of attorney in the desk, signed by his father, verified by the notary. . . .

He stood still suddenly. Santos had told him that the notary was the brother-in-law of Don Belisario. He hadn't seen Don Belisario's wife when he was at La Dorada. He had not even thought of her. But she was the notary's sister, and she was married to Don Belisario, who had a white eye and a white horse. A sudden insight dizzied him.

The power of attorney of which his mother knew

nothing might never have existed before his father's disappearance. But the land had been sold now, and Santa Barbara's men worked there. Tomorrow he would visit Santa Barbara and Doña Isabel, the proud old woman who was used to getting her own way and who still lived there, all alone, in the big house with the tower.

13

The damp room with its smell of musty books oppressed him suddenly. His half-forgotten memories combined with the scraps of stories that he had gleaned here and there made him feel uneasy.

He wanted to know what had happened to his father, but he wasn't sure that he wanted to know everything. Still, how could he ever untangle the mystery of that terrible night, how could he ever know who those men had been, if he was afraid of the shadow of the past?

Why should he be afraid? Because of what Transito and Santos had told him? Because of the way Don Belisario had looked at him with his one eye; the way Blanca had given him her knowing little smile?

He left the room and strode through quiet passageways and across dark patios, down the driveway and along the road to Las Delicias.

The sky was cloudy and the wind moist. Thick drops began to fall, lukewarm drops that pattered on the leaves of the shrubbery by the roadside. Murmuring, the rains came over the parched land. It was the beginning of the rainy season, as Juan de la Cruz had been predicting. It began to rain harder. The road grew muddy, and Carlos Arturo sought shelter under the thick, leafy crown of a *higuerón* tree.

He stood in the warm darkness, listening to the steady murmur of the rain, staring at the empty road, a gray, muddy streak. Nothing else.

Suddenly he heard a slight sound in the bushes behind him. He turned. At first he saw nothing, but when his eyes adjusted to the deeper darkness there, he could make out a dark figure squatting behind the trunk of the *higuerón*. Gradually he saw more . . . a woman holding a bottle, a bottle without a neck, half filled with some pale fluid. Suddenly the realization of who she was dawned on him. Ana-Amanda, who made the trees bleed and caught their white sap in a little bottle without a neck, who looked for herbs in the dead of night and brewed her magic potions in her hut among the rocks at the other side of the lake. A woman who could see the future and the past. Should he speak to her? She was nearby. What should he ask her? He hesitated.

The rain stopped, and more quickly than one would have expected of an old woman, Ana-Amanda stood up. Leaves rustled faintly, a few branches moved, and Ana-Amanda was gone. Carlos Arturo stood and listened. He heard nothing more. Shrugging his shoulders, he continued his way. The path was now a pool of mud. In the distance he saw the uncertain light of the little bar. Coming closer he saw horses standing outside and heard a hubbub of voices within. Las Delicias was full of customers drinking beer, and Blanca was opening bottle after bottle for them. Carlos Arturo did not want to go in. The men only would look at him and fall silent. Blanca would have no time for him. He turned around, a little disappointed. He would have liked to have had a chat with Blanca that evening, about Don Belisario's wife, for instance, and her brother the notary. He would have liked to have questioned her. Blanca, who knew so much and who had told him about Ana-Amanda. If only he had had the presence of mind to speak to Ana-Amanda. Now she was probably back in her hut among the rocks across the lake.

He walked past the gates of Payande and followed the road to the lake. It was dark along the narrow path through the trees. But the sky above the lake gradually cleared; stars winked here and there among shreds of gray cloud. The thin sickle of the moon disappeared behind the trees.

Along the lakeshore frogs croaked. The reeds rustled, and the surface of the dark water stirred. Was it the wind or had some creature in the depths of the lake moved, gliding through the slimy roots of the water plants?

The paths along the lake were soggy. Carlos Arturo's boots squelched, and his feet sometimes sank into the mud. The bushes grew sparser and a dark, jagged wall of rock rose toward the sky with its ragged clouds. The path ascended between big boulders. The ground was solid now beneath his feet. The narrow path forked again and again. A maze of little lanes led to the house of Ana-Amanda.

There. Carlos Arturo stood still. There was the hut, dark in the shadow of the rock wall. The bushes around it dripped. He smelled refuse and rotten leaves. The same old oppressive feeling came over him. Through a crack in the door he saw soft, yellow light, and he heard voices.

"I can't do anything for you now. You know that."

"But I. . . ."

"It's not possible. Not now."

"I have eggs and a candle. . . ."

"Why did you not pay heed to the moon, Virgen Santa?"

"I thought that. . . ."

"Ah, it's always the same, always the same. Leave me in peace."

"But I. . . ." The conversation was drowned out suddenly by the earsplitting screeching of a parrot.

Carlos Arturo did not hear the door open. He heard no footsteps. But he saw a dark shadow vanish among the great gray rocks.

The light went out, and the parrot kept shrieking. He stayed for a while without moving, in the shadow of the rocks, looking at the dark hut. The parrot stopped screeching. Nothing else happened. Slowly, with a pounding heart, he walked to the door. He called. There was no answer. He called again louder. All remained quiet.

Cautiously he opened the door a crack, and immediately the parrot began to screech again. He felt as if something in the hut moved . . . just as, a while ago, something had moved in the dark water of the lake. But he could not see anything. He felt in his pocket for matches and lighted one with a scratch. He entered.

It was close in the hut, and there was a bitter smell. Bundles of herbs hung on the wall, and everywhere stood rusty cans and gray bottles. In a corner he saw a big earthen pot filled with a brown brew. The match burned out. He lighted another one. The big gaudy parrot shifted nervously about on a curtain rod. Ana-Amanda was nowhere to be seen. Again he had the feeling that something was moving in the farthest corner of the room. A huge turtle shuffled slowly from underneath a rickety table.

The threadbare curtain that portioned off a part of

the hut rippled. With a nervous glance at the parrot, who was shuffling on the curtain rod and working his beak, Carlos Arturo crossed the hut in a few rapid steps and jerked aside the curtain. The small space behind it was taken up by a coffin.

Quickly he let the curtain fall again. The match had burned out. It was a while before his trembling fingers were able to light another one. But he really did not want to see anything more. He wanted to leave. His glance fell on the rickety table. A bunch of fresh herbs lay on it and beside them stood a neckless bottle, filled a quarter full with white sap. There were also some eggs and a candle.

Hastily, before the match could burn out, he left the little oppressive hut. The parrot began to screech again, and the turtle scrabbled in a corner. As quickly as he could he sought his way along the little paths that bordered the dark, still lake.

Where, he thought, where could Ana-Amanda have gone? She had been in the hut. He had seen the light. He had heard her talk to someone. Or had he just imagined her? But he had seen the eggs and the candle on the rickety table, beside the fresh herbs and the neckless bottle.

He shivered involuntarily and hastened his steps. The power of Ana-Amanda was great. Was it true what the people said of her . . . true after all?

The shabby hut with its oppressive atmosphere and the stupefying bitter smell had made a deep impression on him. More so than he wanted to acknowledge. He had been afraid of the shuffling old gray turtle and the parrot on the curtain rod. He had been shocked at the sight of the black coffin behind the ragged curtain. A gleaming, black coffin with copper handles, which Ana-Amanda obviously kept there waiting.

14

The sloping lawns of Santa Barbara were smooth and green. Softly tinted oleander flowers blossomed everywhere as well as yellow *copa de oro* and blood-red poinsettias. A waterfall of bougainvillea in different colors, from white to deep purple, covered the scattered stones imbedded in the green of the lawn. It all looked well cared for and impressive.

Carlos Arturo dismounted and tied his horse to a post. He stared at the house. There was no one in sight. Only a bird hopped over the lawn and flew off between the trees. Carlos Arturo lingered. There it was, the house with the tower, standing in the shadow of an enormous old mango tree.

With its overhanging roof, the house looked cool and forbidding. The double doors and the shutters were all closed, as if no one lived there. But at that moment one of the doors opened and a little old lady in a black, long-sleeved dress stepped out on the veranda and peered at him. Then she descended the broad stone steps with the help of a cane and came slowly toward Carlos Arturo across the lawn.

"How nice," she said, when she reached him at last, "there you are. I was wondering where you've been."

"I . . . I'm from Payande. . . ." faltered Carlos Arturo. The little old lady nodded. "Of course," she said. "From Payande. But you know I always worry when you stay out so long. What with the river so near and the narrow path. You never know. And the lake! It's so large and so deep that it always frightens me." She nodded again and gave a fleeting smile.

For a moment Carlos Arturo didn't know what to answer. At last he said, "I am Carlos Arturo, of Payande. I've come to visit you. We're back."

Doña Isabel took a step forward. Leaning on her cane, she peered attentively at Carlos Arturo.

"But, of course. It isn't possible. I got mixed up. It happens sometimes. It's probably because . . . never mind. It happens as one grows older." She smiled again vaguely.

Carlos Arturo did not answer immediately. He felt ill at ease. Doña Isabel was quite frail. He had imagined her quite differently, a proud old woman, domineering and stern. Not like this.

"So you are Carlos Arturo, the son of Raúl." Doña Isabel nodded. "Of course. Now I know. I didn't recognize you immediately. You've grown so. You used to come here in the old days. Many people came then. They don't anymore. It's very quiet now."

With a frail, veined hand she smoothed her forehead. "Won't you come in for a moment? I'm an old woman. I can't stand for long."

She did not wait for an answer but preceded Carlos Arturo to the house. Inside it was dim and cool. Doña Isabel sat down in a wicker rocking chair and motioned him to sit down opposite her. The room was high and wide. The heavy old furniture, the gold chairs, the wood of the red-velvet sofa, and the round tables all shone immaculately. The floor gleamed. The long mirrors sparkled. Enormous family portraits hung on the walls.

Carlos Arturo looked around. The house was very old but beautifully preserved. In a deep recess he saw the stone steps of a winding staircase leading to the tower.

"So you are living again at Payande," said Doña Isabel.

"Yes," replied Carlos Arturo. "We are back, my mother and I."

"Your father came here often," said Doña Isabel slowly. "He liked to sit with me and talk. He liked to talk about the people and their way of life. He would get very excited." She shook her head. "The last time he came he shouted at me. He always had a loud voice, even as a boy. I don't like people to shout at me. It upsets me." She looked disapproving. "He could be very willful and stubborn, but I believe he meant well. Perhaps he was right. Now I often think so, and it frightens me." She made a helpless gesture. "But I am old," she added. "In my time everything was different. When my father lived"—she gave her vague smile—"my father, Don Fausto. You must have heard of him!"

Carlos Arturo nodded.

"He was severe, but just. Like a father to all his people. I always respected that. I submitted to his wishes. I couldn't guess how it would turn out. But you can't foresee everything, can you?" She looked at Carlos Arturo as if she wanted him to agree. He nodded again.

"But Raúl often said that things could not go on this way. Changes would have to come. The people must be awakened out of their passive dependence. That made me angry. But now I think sometimes that he was right . . . now I'm often afraid, especially at night. Soledad won't believe me when I tell her. No, she won't believe me. She thinks I'm just saying something, and she tries to hush me and tells me I have dreamed it, that I'm mixed up." She bent forward in her rocking chair and looked intensely at Carlos Arturo. "But it is not a dream," she said with emphasis. "I *see* it. And I remember it very well." She let herself fall back in her chair again, worn and helpless. "Sometimes," she said in a low voice. "Sometimes. Not always."

Carlos Arturo fidgeted on his chair. He did not know what to say. He had pictured the visit to Doña Isabel quite differently. He did not know how to start talking about the land. He cleared his throat.

"Santa Barbara looks well," he began. "The harvest seems good."

Doña Isabel gave a weary nod. "Santa Barbara has always been a good hacienda. It is fertile land," she said.

"Payande too," said Carlos Arturo. "I am sorry my Uncle Ernesto sold pieces of it." He looked at Doña Isabel. She nodded absently.

"That's the way it goes," she said. She leaned her head against the high wicker back of her chair and closed her eyes. Footsteps sounded inside the house. A door creaked open, a band of sunlight fell into the room and a tough, squat woman appeared. Her long black hair had been combed away from her face and hung in a stiff plait down her back. Her arms and legs were bare and muscular, and the toes of her feet spread out.

"Is anything the matter, Soledad?" asked Doña Isabel without moving.

"No, *señora*," answered Soledad. "I only came to look. I thought I heard voices, that I heard you talking."

"I am not talking. Leave me alone," snapped the old lady. She still leaned back against the chair with her eyes closed. Soledad lingered. She looked from Doña Isabel to Carlos Arturo and back again.

"You are tired," she told Doña Isabel.

"Yes, I am tired," Doña Isabel admitted. Suddenly she sounded resigned.

"*Mi señora*, your grace had better rest," Soledad urged. "You must not excite yourself, or you won't sleep tonight and you'll have bad dreams again, remember?"

"Yes," said Doña Isabel. She got up obediently, smiling vaguely at Carlos Arturo. "Nice of you to come, very nice. You must come more often. In the old days many people came here. But no more. Now no one comes, except at night." Her voice faded away. Leaning on her cane, and followed by the maid, she disappeared into her bedroom.

Carlos Arturo got up. He was lingering, not knowing what to do, when Soledad came back.

"She is getting old, poor soul," she said, shaking her head. "Sometimes she is completely muddled. Then she thinks someone has visited her in the night, someone who wants to harm her. . . ." Soledad hesitated. "But I always lock everything up in the evening when I light the candles before Santa Barbara. And I never forget that." Again she hesitated. Her eyes sought the patron saint of the house in the niche near the winding staircase. "I never forget to light the candles to her," she whispered, "and yet, in the morning, they sometimes are blown out, and then the *señora* is very upset."

They both looked at the old, ornately decorated little altar. Santa Barbara, in a blue dress, stood in a scalloped niche between high carved pillars, three at each side. The wood was artistically sculptured into vines and bunches of grapes. The gilt had flaked here and there, but the altar glowed richly. At the feet of the statue, among the folds of the dress, lay all sorts of dusty articles, mementos of a faraway past. On each side stood two high brass candlesticks holding half-burned candles.

"She talks more and more about Don Fausto, her father, may he rest in peace. When I try to comfort her and tell her she has been dreaming, she gets angry." Soledad sighed.

"When she first saw me today, I think she thought I was my father," said Carlos Arturo haltingly.

Soledad gave him a searching look. "You are from Payande, aren't you?"

Carlos Arturo nodded, and Soledad shook her head again.

"She lives more and more in the past. That is the only time she remembers well. Everything about her father and her husband and her daughter. The rest does not interest her. Only the past."

"She told me that my father often came here and that they argued with each other." Carlos Arturo watched Soledad's expression, but the broad flat face with the high cheekbones remained impassive. She showed no reaction.

"I wonder what they argued about. Doña Isabel said that he shouted at her sometimes." Again he looked at Soledad. He fell silent. He waited tensely.

Soledad nodded. "That's it," she said. "The past. That's what she remembers."

15

"Well," said Juan de la Cruz, "if the *señora* wants to go to the village. . . . But the road is getting very bad now, and the jeep is old. That's the way it is! It's not much good anymore. Especially now the rainy season has started." He shook his old head. "But of course, if we wait longer, the road will get worse. That is true. And I need parts for the generator. I can't make it work, otherwise. And the *señora* needs light."

"We also need rolls of barbed wire for the fences between the pastures," Carlos Arturo added.

"And the supplies have to be replenished," said Doña Luisa. The woman who was cooking for the workers in the shed had been reminding her about the supplies constantly. "And the roof has to be repaired." She suppressed a sigh. Everything was so neglected, she did not know where to start. She had to go to the bank, to the notary, and perhaps have another talk with the judge. All that red tape took such a long time. Over six years had gone by since her husband disappeared, and still the succession rights on the legacy hadn't been settled. One day the matter had to come to an end, and then the taxes would fall due.

"Tell the maids to put the baskets in the jeep," she told Juan de la Cruz. "And ask Transito what we need. Coffee, matches, kerosene. . . ."

In the village Carlos Arturo felt the same uneasiness he had experienced on their arrival. There were the men in the square again, silently observing them. The conversations in little shops stopped when they entered. The notary, in his liquor store, studied his manicured nails as they passed.

Juan de la Cruz wandered off to look for the spare parts he needed, and Doña Luisa said, "Why don't you take care of the shopping list, Carlos Arturo? Then we'll be finished sooner."

"What will you do then?" asked Carlos Arturo.

"I have to speak to some people and go to the bank. . . ."

Carlos Arturo said nothing and did not look at her when she crossed the square. He knew his mother was going to the notary. When he had finished shopping he entered the taproom of the hotel, which was cater-cornered to the notary's liquor store. He ordered coffee and stared across the square.

"Well," said a voice. "If that isn't the son of Raúl—Raúl of Payande."

Carlos Arturo looked up. Before him stood a heavy old man, wearing a faded sport shirt. His stomach bulged over a pair of striped pajama trousers, and his bare feet were stuck into threadbare slippers. He pulled out a chair and sat down. His puffy hands, freckled with liver spots, rested on the table.

"My cognac," he told the waiter. He looked at Carlos Arturo from under bushy gray eyebrows.

"Raúl's son," he said again.

"Yes," answered Carlos Arturo.

"What's your name again?"

"Carlos Arturo."

"Carlos Arturo. That's right. Now I remember. It's so long since I was last at Payande. I used to come often. I knew your father well, very well." He shook his head sadly and ordered another cognac. "A pity, the way things worked out. He was a brilliant man. A pity he did not stay in the city and start a practice there. He would have been a famous doctor. But his heart was in Payande."

"Yes," agreed Carlos Arturo. He looked at the fat old man. There was something familiar about him, although Carlos Arturo could not place him.

"He always looked me up when he came to the village, for he kept up his interest in medical science, and he liked to talk about it."

"That's right," Carlos Arturo said, still trying to identify this man, who talked so familiarly of his father.

"Whenever I came to Payande I always had to go first to the dispensary he had set up there. Not that I believe it was much of a success. The people here are too distrustful and apathetic. I'm confronted with that daily in my practice." He emptied his glass and beckoned impatiently for another. The waiter hastened to shove it to him over the table.

"But what's the use?" the fat man said. "That's the way it is. You can't break iron with your hands. Your father thought otherwise. He was an idealist and a man of action. He was a brilliant young man with a searching mind. We talked a lot together. Our discussions in his study sometimes lasted till deep in the night. Sometimes I ask myself if there wasn't some truth in those theories of his. But what's the use? The people are too frightened and submissive. There is nothing to be done with them. That's what I say. You can't change them." He tugged at his pajama trousers and beckoned the waiter again.

"And you," he asked, looking at Carlos Arturo, "what do you want to drink?"

"I had some coffee."

"Coffee is bad for your heart," said the old man with disapproval. He folded his fat hands carefully around his glass and sipped his cognac.

A girl appeared at the door of the taproom. She

looked around timidly and came slowly toward the little table. "Doctor," she said.

The old man looked up with annoyance. "Yes," he said.

"My mother asks if you'll come. . . ."

"Yes," said the old man again. His bare foot fished under the table for the slipper that had fallen off. But he remained leaning against the table, his hands around his glass.

At the other end of the square the jeep had stopped in front of the notary's liquor store from which Doña Luisa was emerging. Carlos Arturo rose. He shook hands with the old doctor.

"I have to go," he said. "We're ready and have to go back to Payande."

"Payande, I often used to visit there. Your father was a great man. He was a dear friend of mine. A very dear friend. A pity, a great pity," murmured the old man into his empty glass. Wrapped in thought, he remained motionless.

Before they left the village the first thick drops fell. In the dark, leafy tunnel by the bridge they saw that the river had risen. The water foamed over the bridge deck. They were nearly home before Carlos Arturo remembered why the doctor seemed familiar. He had seen him, younger, more robust, and less dilapidated, in the photographs in his father's old-fashioned desk.

16

Blanca was standing in the middle of the muddy road when he passed. She was holding a little boy by the hand.

"Have you heard the news?" she asked. "The bridge has been washed away!"

Carlos Arturo stopped the jeep. "I know," he said. "They came to tell us this morning."

"You went to the village just in time, didn't you?"

"How did you know that?"

Blanca laughed. "I saw you," she said. "I saw you come back too. You had Pablo Pato with you."

"That's right," admitted Carlos Arturo testily. They had been driving back in the pouring rain when, just outside the village, the man had asked for a lift.

"I didn't know he was free again," said Blanca.

"What do you mean, *free?*"

Blanca looked at him. "Don't you know?" she asked. "Pablo Pato stuck a knife in someone's ribs a couple of months ago."

"Is that so?" said Carlos Arturo curtly. He felt annoyed that Blanca knew so much more about the people around Laguna Grande than he. "Perhaps he was innocent, and they let him go," he suggested.

Blanca laughed derisively. "Of course he wasn't innocent. They knew right away he'd done it and took him to the scene of his crime. Then he began to cry."

"Cry?"

"Yes, the murderer always cries at the scene of his crime. Didn't you know that?"

"No, I never heard such nonsense," said Carlos Arturo bluntly.

Blanca laughed again. "Where are you going?" she asked.

"To Venetië, to take the rolls of barbed wire Sabas needs."

"Oh." Blanca lingered. She kept looking at him, her body swaying gently.

"And where are *you* going?

"I'm on an errand for my mother."

"Would you like a lift?"

"I might," said Blanca, her eyes gleaming. "The road is so muddy with all this rain." She lifted the small boy into the jeep and got in herself.

"Where do you want to go?"

"In the direction of Santa Barbara."

"To Santa Barbara? What are you going to do there?"

"A message from my mother," Blanca repeated.

He did not ask anything further and drove past the path to Venetië in the direction of Santa Barbara. "Is that your brother?" he asked, to make conversation.

"He's sick," said Blanca. "He hasn't been well for a long time."

Carlos Arturo looked at the bare, muddy feet of the child who sat silent and resigned between them. "Why do you take him with you then?" he asked. "In the mud, with his bare feet."

"He's sick," Blanca said again. They approached the stone ridge where the road became narrow and slowly mounted before its descent toward Santa Barbara.

"You can put me off here," said Blanca. He stopped. Blanca got out and lifted the little boy from the jeep.

"Where are you going then?" asked Carlos Arturo again, though he knew the answer now.

"Fetching medicine from Ana-Amanda." Triumphantly Blanca pushed the little boy ahead of her on the narrow, much-trodden footpath between high shrubbery and the great stones. Carlos Arturo saw the red of her dress bob among the green and disappear behind a slope of the stone ridge.

Slowly he pulled the jeep to the side of the road and followed. She pretended not to notice, but when she reached the open space where the hut stood, she looked over her shoulder. She did not say anything, but Carlos Arturo stopped involuntarily.

Ana-Amanda was busy in her yard. She was half hidden by the smoke of the caldron. The parrot on the edge of the partly open door began to screech, and Ana-Amanda, with an imperious movement of her hand, turned and looked at Blanca and the little boy.

"My mother sent me," said Blanca, shuffling her feet. All the cockiness had gone out of her. Her voice sounded submissive. The old woman did not speak, but kept looking at the little boy.

"She sends greetings," Blanca added haltingly.

Ana-Amanda nodded. She threw a piece of wood on the fire. Then she straightened and stood there in the smoke, upright and somber in her dark clothes, enveloped in a ring of smoke.

Something rustled among the bushes with the strange cupped flowers. Branches stirred. The wood under the caldron crackled and settled. Flames licked around the iron pot.

Slowly Ana-Amanda pulled some dried herbs out of the pocket of her black skirt and began to crumble them carelessly between her bony fingers. Then she released the dust, which swirled upward into the thick vapor of the gaping pot, where it precipitated and began to spread a penetrating odor.

Ana-Amanda stood in the bittersweet smoke, a very old woman with a proud bearing and cool commanding eye. The wood flickered and the flames died out.

"Come," said Ana-Amanda to the child. She slowly walked ahead to the hut. Blanca, shoving the child in front of her, followed. The parrot hopped along the edge of the door when they entered. It ruffled its feathers and screeched again.

Carlos Arturo still was standing on the narrow path between the rocks. He stared at the hut, feeling uncomfortable, though nothing remarkable could be seen. The hut was old and darkened by rain, the roof half hidden by a jutting piece of rock. Rubbish lay everywhere. A few ducks and an armadillo with a string around its middle were rooting around. An iguana slid away between the bushes and the rocks.

From the lake came the shrill cry of a heron. No sound came from the hut, where Blanca and the child were with Ana-Amanda. Carlos Arturo kept his eyes fixed on the half-open door. The parrot stopped screeching, and a big gray turtle crawled slowly out of the hut.

Carlos Arturo turned and quickly walked back to the jeep. He drove furiously to Venetië, jumped out in front of Sabas's house and looked around.

"Is Sabas here?" he called, startling the old woman in her chair on the veranda.

Carmencita came hurriedly from the little river where she had been doing the wash on a big stone.

"Where is Sabas?" Carlos Arturo asked again. He looked at Carmencita. Her children had come running and now were pushing shyly around her.

"Sabas?" repeated Carmencita, standing in her yard, encircled by the children. Her body was heavy, her naked legs childish and angular. "Sabas has gone out to the pastures with the big boys."

"Sabas," called the old woman from the veranda. "What are you saying about Sabas? Sabas is a good boy, isn't he, Carmencita?"

Carmencita cast a timid glance at the old woman, slumped in her chair.

"Yes, ma'am," she said meekly.

"He's a good boy. He always looks after his old mother." Her hand stroked the rough leather of her chair. She looked suspiciously at Carlos Arturo.

"Yes, ma'am," Carmencita said again.

"I came to bring the barbed wire," said Carlos Arturo.

"Sabas has gone out to the pastures," repeated Carmencita.

"Have you got a horse here? Then I can ride there. The jeep won't make it in this rain."

"A horse. Go and fetch a horse for Señor Carlos Arturo," Carmencita told one of the little boys, who ran off.

"A horse," babbled the old woman on the porch. "Sabas's horse. Don't sit on it. But Sabas has gone to the pastures with the boys. He's a hard worker. He's a good boy."

"Yes, ma'am. Be quiet now. Señor Carlos Arturo knows that very well," said Carmencita. She looked apologetically at Carlos Arturo.

"She's getting very old, the poor woman," she said in a low voice. "She talks a lot of nonsense, and she can hardly move. I have to help her all the time with everything." One of the small children began to cry, and she bent and lifted him.

The little boy arrived with the horse, which he had caught and saddled for Carlos Arturo. Carlos Arturo mounted, said good-bye, and rode off.

He found Sabas and his sons with the cattle. Sabas came riding toward him, hat in hand. They talked for a moment, and Carlos Arturo told him that he had brought the rolls of barbed wire. "They are lying at Venetië," he said.

"Yes, *señor*," said Sabas.

"Have you been to the quarry for posts?"

"No, *señor*."

"Let's go and look there now. I'd like to see it."

"Yes, *señor*," said Sabas. He shouted a few instructions to his sons, and then they rode together through the pastures, which were marshy with rain. Up the mountains they went through thick shrubbery and coarse wet grass, and now and then they crossed little streams of wildly rushing water.

"You can see that it's been raining hard."

"Yes, *señor*. It is the rainy season."

"Last night the bridge was swept away."

"Yes, *señor*. I heard about it."

How, thought Carlos Arturo. These people lived away in the mountains, yet they knew everything. "We went to the village just in time. The road was bad enough, but now the bridge is gone. . . ."

"Yes, *señor*. The road is bad, very bad," agreed Sabas.

"I met the old doctor in the village. He used to come often to Payande."

Sabas did not answer, and he asked no questions. His face expressed neither emotion nor interest.

"He is in a photograph we have. So are you, with a big zebu, a great blue bull."

"Ah, that was El Gigante," said Sabas. His face lighted up. "He was a good bull," he said. "A very good bull. He's no longer here. A pity."

"Yes, a pity," said Carlos Arturo. "What happened to him?"

"What shall I say, *señor?* He was dead when we found him one day. He was old."

Carlos Arturo did not ask any further questions. Perhaps the animal had grown ill, perhaps he had had an accident and they had butchered him, or perhaps he had been stolen or sold. Carlos Arturo never would hear anything more about El Gigante than that they had found him dead one day.

They rode on. The sky over the mountains was dark and threatening. It began to rain. Sabas wrapped himself in a sheet of plastic, which he had pulled out from behind his saddle. In single file they rode through the wet bushes along the slippery slopes. All around them was the gray of the rain, the splash of water on branches and leaves, the gurgling of creeks. Gradually new streams were forming everywhere.

"I'm sopping wet," said Carlos Arturo.

"Yes, *señor*, and the weather isn't getting any better," said Sabas in a resigned voice. Carlos Arturo tugged at the collar of his shirt where the water dribbled down his back. He realized how far they were from the shelter of Venetië and the big house.

Then he remembered El Cojo's hut and changed the direction of his horse.

After a while Sabas called, "This is not the way to the quarry, *señor*."

"I know. I want to take shelter at El Cojo's."

"At El Cojo's, *señor?*"

"Yes, he lives around here somewhere. It can't be far." He shivered in his wet clothes and peered into the gray of the falling rain.

"It should be about here," he said.

There was an open space fenced in with rusty barbed wire. The ground sloped away to a narrow river. They heard the wild roaring of water over boulders. Inside the fence stood an old sagging hut, black with rain. Carlos Arturo dismounted and brought his horse into the fenced yard. It was silent there. He saw no one, and there was no trace of animals. No dogs, no chickens, no hoof marks of horses in the mud. Nothing at all.

When he opened the crooked door, which at once fell shut behind him, a thick, fetid smell met him. The hut was empty and dim, but it was dry. When his eyes got used to the gloom, he discovered a heap of black, rotten straw in a corner. It looked as if it had been a mattress. There was no other furniture. Only in the lean-to kitchen, less dark because its back door was missing, he saw a rusty pan standing over ashes on some stones. And on a plank against the wall he saw a stump of candle in a dented enamel mug.

Carlos Arturo looked around. Clearly no one had lived there for a long time. He stood in the gap of the missing door. It was still raining, but here he was dry and breathed fresh air. He looked over the muddy, deserted yard. He saw a gap in the fence and a path that led to the river. He heard water beating against rocks.

It kept raining, and he realized suddenly that Sabas had not followed him. He walked back through the stinking hut and pushed open the door that had fallen shut behind him.

Sabas was sitting motionless on his horse, just outside the fence, shoulders hunched together, rain beating against his face. Water dripped from his big hat onto the folds of the plastic. He did not react when Carlos Arturo called to him, and the door creaked shut again.

As he walked back to the kitchen, where the air was less oppressive, he saw an upturned wooden crate with an unsightly dirty pouch on it. The pouch looked familiar, and he went to it, touching a corner cautiously. Yes, it was the pouch of knotted string in which El Cojo kept the pottery that he found in old Indian graves. The same pouch that he took with him when he visited his father. It was moldy and rotted and very dirty. Carlos Arturo shoved it off the crate with his foot and tried to pull it apart with the toe of his boot. He didn't succeed, so he picked up the stump of candle and lighted it. He squatted near the loathsome brown rag. It stank and was alive with maggots, but it fascinated him. He held the candle closer and kept looking.

At last he rose, and then his glance fell on the top of the crate, which had been hidden by the pouch. In the soft wood, letters had been scratched. Difficult, angular letters, scarcely readable. He spelled them out slowly: *E-d-e-l-l-o-G-a-s-i-n-t-o-S-a-v-a-s*. He looked from the letters to the bundle and back to the letters. He had an impulse to put the stinking rag back on the crate, but his stomach began to heave. The sickening stench in the hut became unbearable. He walked through the gap of the missing kitchen door into the yard.

It was not pouring any longer, though there was still a drizzle. Everything around was black and drenched with water. He flung the stump of candle far away. It fell in the mud near the gap in the fence and the path that led to the river. He waded around the hut to his horse. On the other side of the fence Sabas still sat, motionless, hunched on his horse, waiting.

17

"Do you know what happened to him?" asked Carlos Arturo.

"Yes, *señor*. They found him in the river," said Juan de la Cruz. He was sitting on the floor of the engine room, fiddling with the motor. "It won't go," he muttered. "This pesky generator is too old."

"In the river?" repeated Carlos Arturo. "Did he drown?"

"Yes, *señor*. He drowned."

"How did it happen? Was it an accident?"

"An accident," agreed Juan de la Cruz. "It must have been. He must have lost his balance and fallen in. He was old, you know, and he had only one leg. That was the cause of it all, that one leg."

"It was a horrible accident, the one at the sugar mill," agreed Carlos Arturo.

Juan de la Cruz searched for a while among the nuts and bolts on the floor. Then he said slowly, "It would have been better if Don Raúl, your father, had not interfered."

"What?" said Carlos Arturo. "If my father hadn't interfered, El Cojo would have died."

"Then he would have been no worse off than he is now. And at least he would have had his leg still. Just like Sabas's mother. She's been ailing for years since her fall. But she still has both her legs, even though they're useless."

"But it was different with El Cojo," said Carlos Arturo impatiently. "His whole foot was infected, and his leg was swollen. Don't you remember how he looked when they found him up there in the hut? They had to carry him away in a stretcher."

"Yes," admitted Juan de la Cruz. "And later, when he came back, he had only one leg."

A shadow fell on the floor of the engine room. Transito stood in the doorway. "That's right," she said. "He would have been better off if he had stayed here. He had Ana-Amanda to help him. What does a strange doctor in the city know about us?" The corners of her mouth drooped.

Carlos Arturo turned and left. Maids passed him with lighted oil lamps. The soft yellow light danced along the halls and wet patios, where the water gurgled in the gutters. It had been raining steadily. They heard the water patter in the cisterns around the house. Inside drops fell with monotonous regularity into the pots and cans that had been put under the cracks in the ceiling. The roof was leaking everywhere. Now and then a piece of plaster fell with a plop.

Carlos Arturo entered his father's study. A lamp stood on the table. In a corner above the bookcase there was another leak. Slowly he began to pull the books out of the bookcase to save them from the water. He put them in piles on the table. They were his father's textbooks and discolored notebooks, the ink on them blotted here and there. They looked pathetic: old, much-read books, half out of their bindings, with yellowed pages. Bits of paper that served as bookmarks stuck out of some of them. Absently he arranged the books on the big, square table. Everything was clammy and moist. He felt cold and shivery.

That evening his mother and he ate their dinner silently and went to their rooms early.

It kept raining that whole night. Carlos Arturo could not get to sleep. The rain fell in streams. Far away the river roared, and the night hung gray and threatening at the windows. Just like the night that his father . . . the sound of horses galloping away.

He listened, but everything was still, dead still, except for the rain.

Who were those men who had abducted his father? What had they done with him? What had happened to El Cojo—El Cojo who had known!

An accident, Juan de la Cruz had called it. "He was old and had only one leg."

An old man, in a lonely hut. Someone who could not defend himself. Had he heard them come, one night in the dark, when he was lying on his litter in a corner of the hut? Had he known who they were?

Did they come because he had warned Don Raúl? Were they the same men who had abducted his father? But during the investigation, in the months that they had searched unceasingly for his father, El Cojo had kept quiet.

"Hush, not one of us has seen anything." Those were the words of Transito. No one knew anything. Only El Cojo, who had drowned, like Edelio. Carlos Arturo sat up straight in bed. Just like Edelio. . . . Edelio, Jacinto, and Sabas!

No, that was nonsense. Jacinto was not drowned. Jacinto sat dazed and vacant in Santos's dark hut.

How did he come to think of Jacinto and Sabas? Edelio, Jacinto, and Sabas. Those were the names scratched on the top of the crate in El Cojo's hut. El Cojo, who had known that he owed his life to Don Raúl, no matter what people said. Who often had come to them on Payande. He never had gone back to Santa Barbara. To Doña Isabel in her big house, in the midst of her lands and the land of Payande that had been sold by power of attorney. A power of attorney found in a drawer of his father's desk when they needed money. His lips curled. He didn't doubt for a moment that the notary of the village had profited by this transaction. The notary, who was Don Belisario's brother-in-law. Don Belisario had hated his father. What would he care if Payande was ruined? There was no one now who could stop him from putting a dam in a river if he wanted to. No one to threaten him.

There was that accident at the bridge, when Don Belisario in his anger had turned too abruptly and his son was killed.

"So many accidents at the bridge," Blanca had said. Now the bridge had been swept away by the water. They were shut off from the world. Isolated, completely isolated.

And the rain kept falling.

18

Juan de la Cruz appeared in the doorway of the dining room. He waited with his hat in his hand. He was wet through.

Outside it was gray with rain. The road was a pool of mud. The grass in the fields stood in water that the ground could not absorb anymore. Here and there groups of people, with their scanty possessions, were fleeing to higher ground. The people were coming from the direction of the lake.

"What's the matter, Juan de la Cruz?" asked Doña Luisa.

"What shall I say, *señora?* The fields near Sabas, on Venetië, are flooded. And my daughter, Carmencita, his wife, is feeling bad. It is her time. And with all this water, and the children, and Sabas's mother, who sits in her chair and cannot move."

Doña Luisa rose.

"It's bad weather," Juan de la Cruz continued. "It keeps raining. I've never seen it so bad."

"Yes, it's terrible," agreed Doña Luisa. "They can't stay at Venetië. They must come here. It's safer here. Can't you fetch Carmencita in the jeep?"

"Yes, *señora*," said Juan de la Cruz.

"I'll go with you," offered Carlos Arturo.

The fields of Venetië were flooded. The children huddled in the mud on the veranda. The dogs, the pigs, and the chickens wandered through the house. Sabas had pulled his mother's chair inside the door. The old woman sagged, crooked and powerless, in the doorway, blocking the way.

In the farthest corner of the house Carmencita lay on a bed behind a curtain.

"We've come with the jeep," said Carlos Arturo. He looked shyly at Sabas. "Can she walk to it?"

"Carmencita, get up!" ordered Sabas impatiently. "Here is Señor Carlos Arturo with the jeep."

"Yes, *señor*," muttered Carmencita meekly. She appeared from behind the curtain.

"Can you sit in front?" asked Carlos Arturo.

"And what happens to my mother?" asked Sabas. "She can't walk anymore."

"We can carry her to the jeep," Carlos Arturo proposed. "Juan de la Cruz is here too. We can manage with the three of us."

"Ah, what is happening to me! Where is my chair?

My chair!" moaned the old woman as the three of them lugged her to the jeep. Juan de la Cruz chased the children into the back of the jeep.

"My chair! Where is my chair?" the old woman complained from the front of the jeep.

"Hush, ma'am, we're going to the big house. It's dry there, with many chairs," said Carmencita shyly.

"We can come back later for the furniture," said Carlos Arturo. He looked at Carmencita. She sat on the hard front seat, the heavy body of the old woman leaning against her.

"Sabas can come back with the jeep. The big boys can help him."

Slowly they drove to Payande. Groups of men stood together in the yard. Doña Luisa appeared.

"We have everything ready for Carmencita in one of the outbuildings," she said hurriedly. "Her mother is there already, and Transito and the maids are boiling water." She brushed a strand of hair from her face with the back of her hand.

The old woman was lifted out of the jeep. Carmencita and the children disappeared into one of the outbuildings. Sabas and Juan de la Cruz drove off again in the jeep.

Blanca stood under an overhang. "So Carmencita has come. You've gone and fetched her in the jeep. It's her time, I suppose."

"Yes." Carlos Arturo nodded. "It's her time."

"I suppose she'll leave when the child is born."

Carlos Arturo expected too that Sabas would leave after Carmencita's child was born. "Why should they leave?" he snapped. "Sabas has worked here for a long time."

"Ah," said Blanca scornfully, "but they are all afraid."

"Afraid?" asked Carlos Arturo. "And why has Juan de la Cruz stayed here all these years, and Transito?"

"Ah," Blanca said again. "Transito is different. Nothing can happen to Transito since she saw the face of the virgin on the stone where she sharpens knives." Carlos Arturo was silent. He knew that Transito kept a stone in her room, a stone with the face of the virgin on it. The features were scarcely to be distinguished, but all the same. . . .

"And Juan de la Cruz then . . ." he said in an attempt to defend himself, to defend Payande.

Blanca shrugged her shoulders. "The mother of Juan de la Cruz and the mother of Transito were sisters. Twins. That's why."

Carlos Arturo didn't answer. He stared over the muddy grounds, and at the rain. He saw the jeep come back. He saw his mother and Transito walk into the house. He followed them. Transito brought coffee.

"It's terrible," she said. "I never have seen such

weather! More and more people are coming from the lake below."

"I'm worried about Doña Isabel," Doña Luisa said quietly. "So old and alone in that big house."

"Yes, poor soul. She is old." Transito nodded. "And the house is on lower ground, lower than Payande."

"Perhaps you could go to her." Doña Luisa looked hesitatingly at Carlos Arturo. "You never know. Perhaps you can persuade her to come back with you. With you and Soledad. She's old and absolutely alone . . . with all this rain!"

She kept looking at Carlos Arturo. The rain fell in streams. In the house the water dripped incessantly into pails and buckets.

Transito took the empty cups away. "If the master still can get through," she said.

19

Rain beat against the windshield of the jeep. Carlos Arturo hardly could see anything. Slowly he drove to Santa Barbara. The lower parts of the road were flooded. The wheels splashed through the water and spun through the mud. He shifted gears. The jeep went on.

There was the house, gray in the rain. The sky, the land, the road, everything was gray. The mountains were not to be seen. The jeep sank into a deep hole. The water rose above the axles. The mud sucked, the wheels spun, the motor rattled and stopped. In the silence that followed he heard only the whisper of the rain and the distant roar of the Río Tigre.

A flash of lightning split the monotonous gray, and from over the mountains waves of thunder rumbled nearer. Carlos Arturo tried to start the motor again, but without success. He waited a bit and tried again, still without success.

He looked around in the jeep for something to cover himself, but found nothing. So, bent over, his shoulders hunched, he left the jeep and ran to the house.

Soledad stood in the big kitchen. "Did you come to see Doña Isabel?" she asked. "In this weather?"

"My mother sent me," Carlos Arturo answered. "She's worried about how she's getting along in this rain. I came to check for her."

Soledad shook her head. "You can't see the *señora*," she said. "She is very upset again. No, the *señora* can't receive anybody."

Carlos Arturo sat down on a stool at the table. "The jeep has stuck in the mud. It's standing in the road there. I'll have to wait till the rain lets up a bit."

There was another flash of lightning. His last words were drowned in the rolling thunderclaps.

Inside the house a voice called. "Soledad!"

"Yes, *señora*."

"Soledad, what is it? I hear voices!"

"Yes, *señora*," Soledad answered again. She hurried out of the kitchen. Carlos Arturo followed behind her slowly.

"It's the young *señor* from Payande," he heard Soledad say. "He's coming to inquire after you."

"The young *señor* from Payande? Has Raúl come

again? He's often impatient. That upsets me. I know, I know he's right, but I can't stand up to her."

"Yes, *señora*, I've already told him you can't receive anyone. But he's stuck here with the jeep. The road is flooded. All this rain is terrible."

"The rain . . ." repeated Doña Isabel. "Yes, it has been raining for a long time. It's bad weather. Ask the young *señor* to come in, Soledad."

"Yes, *señora*." Soledad looked disapprovingly at Carlos Arturo as he entered the big room. It was dark; the shutters were all closed. He saw no one.

"The *señora* is in her bedroom. She isn't well," said Soledad. She waited, and Carlos Arturo approached reluctantly. Doña Isabel sat in her big baroque Spanish bed, propped up among her pillows. Her frail hands moved over the sheet. Around her on bedside tables stood many little pots and bottles and boxes of medicine. There were also some glasses of fruit juice and a plate of untouched food.

"I came to inquire how you are," said Carlos Arturo. "My mother sent me. She is worried about you in this weather." The old woman examined him closely.

"Who are you?" she asked finally.

"I'm Carlos Arturo, from Payande."

She kept looking at him. "Carlos Arturo," she repeated at last. "Of course. I thought you were Raúl. He comes here often. He has warned me many times, but

I can't stand up to her. She knows that." Doña Isabel glanced at Soledad. "No one will believe me. Soledad does not believe me either when I tell her."

Another flash of lightning flickered through the house. Thunder rumbled darkly and slowly rolled away again. The rain hammered on the tiled roof. A gust of wind tugged at the shutters. In the big room the old wood creaked.

Doña Isabel sunk back in her pillows. "Ah," she said, "many is the time I've heard that sound when I can't sleep. Then I know she is here. She is wicked, very wicked, and Raúl is angry. Sometimes he's even angry with me, angry and impatient, and then he shouts at me. I can't stand that. It gives me a headache." She closed her eyes.

"She is quite confused again, poor soul," said Soledad. "It's better for her not to talk so much. She always talks about the past. Sometimes it's about the *señor*, her father. Lord, he's been dead for such a long time! Then she gets excited and restless. It's better to leave her alone."

"Yes," said Carlos Arturo with a timid glance at the frail figure in the bed, the white face, the restless hands.

He sat down in the big room. Soledad lighted a lamp and went away. Carlos Arturo looked aimlessly around the large, shadowy room. Outside the rain kept falling. The thunderstorm drifted away and came rolling back

156

again. It remained hanging over the valley, between the mountains. The wind blew harder and harder. The shutters rattled, the floors creaked, the whole house groaned and squeaked.

Carlos Arturo rose. He ambled through the room where the heavy furniture cast dark shadows. The family portraits moved with the draft. A cold current of air blew down the tower. He mounted the winding staircase. Up there it was dark and chilly, and the noise of the rain and wind was much louder. Raindrops blew in through a broken windowpane. He tried to look out and see the jeep, but it was too dark. Only the lightning lighted the flooded countryside.

He shuffled down again.

Soledad had returned. She stood by the little altar. She was lighting the candles to the patron saint of the house, standing in her gilt niche between the carved pillars.

"I've laid the table for you in the dining room," she said, before she returned to the kitchen.

Carlos Arturo stood irresolute in front of Santa Barbara. He looked at the dusty objects at her feet: empty cartridges, a few discolored epaulettes, a wreath of dried flowers.

Santa Barbara stood on her pedestal in the scalloped niche, the arms lifted in a protective gesture. Her staring eyes were raised to an angel holding a sword over her head. Suddenly Carlos Arturo thought her gesture more defensive than protective.

Turning, he found his way through the dimly lighted house, with its dark corners and narrow, unexpected hallways between yard-thick walls, to the dining room. Soledad brought him soup with meat and rice. He ate hurriedly.

"You can't leave now," said Soledad.

"No, I can't leave in this weather. Everything is flooded." They listened to the rain around the house and the thunder in the distance.

"I've locked the doors," said Soledad. She took the dirty plates to the kitchen. Carlos Arturo returned to the large room and sat down in Doña Isabel's rocking chair. Soledad went once more to look at her mistress. She pushed a glass of fruit juice among the bottles of medicine and took back the plate and dirty glasses.

There was some clatter from the direction of the kitchen. Then everything grew quiet. The humming of the generator stopped. The lights went out.

Carlos Arturo sat in Doña Isabel's chair. He stared into the darkness. Only the niche where the altar stood was faintly lighted by the burning candles. Sometimes lightning shot a blue flare through the room.

The thunderstorm was drifting nearer again, and thunderclaps followed one another more rapidly, rolling like dark waves. It kept raining. The wind blew.

He heard the uneven breathing of the old woman in the bedroom. He rocked gently in her chair. He tried to sleep, but he could not. He felt oppressed, locked up in this strange, big house with its unfamiliar noises. The squeaking of a shutter, the creaking of the floors, the thunderstorm, the rain, the wind, the roaring of the river in the dark of night. The grating of the boulders under the violence of the water.

That was the way it had been the night his father had been abducted. The trampling of hoofs in the front of the house, the dogs that barked and then stopped, the receding footsteps of his father, those quiet reassuring steps. He must have recognized the men even in the dark. He had gone with them as a matter of course, and he never had come back. No trace of him ever had been found. Who had those men been? Men from the neighborhood, workers from Payande.

Edelio, who worked for them then, and Sabas, who lived on Venetië and looked after the cattle, and Jacinto, Santos's son. But why? And who had planned the abduction? Edelio, Jacinto, Sabas—names scratched on the crate in El Cojo's hut. The white hindquarters of a horse in the grayness of the rain . . . the pouring rain.

"I know that you are here," said a voice. "Why don't you go? I'm old. Leave me in peace."

Carlos Arturo started. Had he slept?

The candles before the altar were blown out. The wooden floor creaked.

He half rose in his chair. "Doña Isabel," he said. "I'm here, Carlos Arturo."

"Leave me in peace," Doña Isabel said plaintively. "You're wicked. I know you are. I know everything. Do you hear?"

Fitful blue light flickered through the room. The boards creaked again. Did he see her figure there, in the middle of the room . . . a dark brittle figure? He thought he'd seen her plainly.

"Why are you standing there? Why did you get out of bed?" he asked, terrified.

"I'm here," said Doña Isabel. Her voice came from the bedroom.

Carlos Arturo now rose completely from his chair. Fully awake, with his hands groping before him, he took a few steps in the darkness.

Again lightning flashed through the house.

The room was empty. No one was there. A cold draft brushed past him. Feeling his way, he found the bedroom and searched for the candle he'd seen on one of the tables near the bed. With trembling fingers he struck a match.

Doña Isabel lay sunk away in the pillows, her eyes wide and staring with fear. "You'd better go away now," she said shrilly. "I know everything. It's wicked, wicked what you're doing!"

"It's me, Doña Isabel," said Carlos Arturo. The candle was burning.

"Raúl. . . ." whispered Doña Isabel.

Carlos Arturo let the mistake pass. "You must drink something," he said soothingly. He handed her the glass with fruit juice. He watched as she drank it. She was very excited. Her white hair hung untidily around her face. Her thin fingers nervously clutched the glass. She pushed it away after a few sips.

"You're right," she said. "I know you're right. But it's too late. I'm old and tired. I can't go against it. It's not my fault that it happened this way. My father wanted it. He arranged it. He could be hard, my father, but he was just. He always saw that everyone got what was his due. He arranged it this way. Surely you know that."

She's raving, thought Carlos Arturo. She's ill and raving. He looked at the pale, sunken face with the wide, staring eyes. "I'll call Soledad," he said.

"Soledad," the old woman repeated slowly, as if she were coming to her senses. "Soledad! She won't come in the night. She's afraid." The fingers of her transparent hand clutched the sheets. "I'm afraid too," she said in a small voice.

I'm going to call Soledad anyway, thought Carlos Arturo. I'm not going to stay here alone. He picked up the candlestick.

"Are you going?" asked Doña Isabel.

"I'm going to fetch Soledad," Carlos Arturo answered. "We'll be back."

The old woman didn't answer. She lay deep in her pillows, staring with wide, dilated eyes.

Carlos Arturo walked with the burning candle through the big house, across hollow rooms, past patios where the rain streamed down, along narrow hallways between thick walls.

At last he came to the patio where Soledad slept behind one of the doors. He called her, and in a moment she appeared.

"What is the matter?" she asked.

"You must come right away," said Carlos Arturo.

"I?" Soledad retreated, frightened. "To the big house? At this hour?" she asked, startled.

"Doña Isabel is ill," said Carlos Arturo.

"She is old. She needs peace."

"Come along," Carlos Arturo commanded curtly. He pushed her ahead of him across the patio through the drafty halls and high, empty rooms. The candle blew out. He lighted it again in the big room.

It was silent in the bedroom of the old woman. Only her uneven breathing was audible.

"I think she's asleep again," he said, feeling foolish.

"Yes, she's sleeping," said Soledad.

"But she was very excited, and she was talking to someone."

"She was dreaming," said Soledad.

"I saw a figure too."

"What?" asked Soledad.

They stood facing each other, lost in the great room in the eerie light of the candle.

"I saw someone stand here in the room. I saw a figure plainly." Soledad was silent. She fidgeted.

"I thought at first it was Doña Isabel." When Soledad kept silent, he went on quickly, "But it wasn't. I went and looked. She was in bed. She kept talking. She thought I was my father, and she talked of her own father, Don Fausto."

"Yes." Soledad nodded. "She talks of him often, of her father, Don Fausto." Her eyes inadvertently sought the portrait of Don Fausto among the many stately pictures on the wall. Then her glance fell on the statue of Santa Barbara.

"Look, the candles! They're out!" she whispered.

"Yes, they're out," Carlos Arturo agreed hoarsely.

They stood there motionless. Lightning flashes illumined the room with an iridescent blue light. Rain splashed down, and the wind moaned around the house. A chilly draft came from the tower.

The candle on the table flickered, and the paintings on the wall stirred slightly. The dignified figure of Don Fausto seemed to loosen itself from the past and join them.

20

They stood in the kitchen doorway and gazed over the flooded countryside. In the backyard a group of men on horseback loomed out of the darkness. Their dark figures and grim faces became recognizable. Slowly it grew lighter.

The cattle huddled together on the hilltops, the calves in the midst of them. Water glittered over the whole valley. Everywhere in the mountains small cataracts had formed. There were deep wounds in the green slopes where earth and rocks had been washed away.

The men in the yard talked of the damage the water had done. Cattle had been drowned, huts had been washed away, people were missing. Soledad went back to the kitchen. She poked the fire. She fried *arepas* and made hot chocolate. Carlos Arturo remained standing at the kitchen door, staring into the distance.

On the stone ridge a man appeared on a big white horse, surrounded by workers on their small brown mounts. They were carefully picking their way along the narrow horse trail and came single file through the water to the house.

They were splattered from head to toe with mud. When Carlos Arturo saw Don Belisario, he withdrew into a dark corner of the kitchen.

Don Belisario entered. "How is it here?" he asked Soledad. He took off his sopping leather leggings and let them fall to the floor. "How is Doña Isabel?" He did not wait for an answer but marched straight into the house with great strides.

Soledad hurried after him. "My mistress is bad today," she said. "She is quite confused. Ave María, it's a bad thing to grow so old."

They stood outside the open bedroom door and looked in. Doña Isabel lay apathetically in her pillows, her eyes with the big dark pupils wide open.

"Doña Isabel," said Don Belisario. He entered the room and pulled up a chair by the bed. "Doña Isabel, how are you? I thought after the terrible weather last night I'd better take a look at Santa Barbara. I can't remember a night as bad as this. Whole plots are under water, and many head of cattle were drowned. There have been landslides too. A great deal of damage has been done."

Doña Isabel looked vaguely at him. Don Belisario's words did not seem to register. At last she whispered, "She was here again last night."

Don Belisario did not answer, and Soledad shook her head pityingly. "The *señora* was dreaming again last night," she said to Don Belisario. But she threw a worried glance at the altar in the niche, where Carlos Arturo had withdrawn quietly, and at the candles in front of Santa Barbara, which she had lighted once more.

Doña Isabel kept looking at Don Belisario. "She was here again last night," she repeated. "She comes more and more. She's bad, but her power is great."

Don Belisario bent toward her. "Who is it? Whom are you talking about?"

"Ana-Amanda," said the old woman wearily. "She's a bad woman. Raúl often has warned me against her."

It was very quiet for a moment. Don Belisario stared at her with his one eye. He moved heavily and the chair creaked. "Don Raúl," he said scornfully. "No one need tell me anything about Don Raúl. He was a hothead, and he thought he was master of this valley. But he was no match for Ana-Amanda. She was the only one in the world who did not pay attention to him."

The old woman in the bed kept looking at him intently. Her mouth moved as if she were reading the words from his lips in order to understand them better.

"Raúl knew she was bad," she repeated obstinately. "He often has warned me against the wicked power she has over us, over us all. But what could I do? My father ordained it. My father, Don Fausto. He was just. But he would not have approved of this, that I know. He loved Santa Barbara and this house. Yes, this house. It's been in the family a long time. My grandfather was born here, and my father and I, all of us. And my daughter." She began to stroke the bed sheet nervously. "Yes, she too," she added.

Don Belisario pushed back his chair. "I must go," he said. "Is there anything I can do for you?"

"Tell her not to come again," said Doña Isabel. "I'm old. I'm afraid of her."

Don Belisario shrugged his heavy shoulders. "She won't come now," he said. "Everything is flooded."

"She was here last night," answered Doña Isabel.

"I have to go home," repeated Don Belisario. "To my wife. She just sits there, upstairs, as usual. For years she hasn't come down. The doctors say it was the shock. She never got over it. She just sits there. That's the way it is. There's nothing to be done about it."

Involuntarily Carlos Arturo drew farther back into the shadows of the altar. He hoped Don Belisario would not start talking about his father again. He hoped Don Belisario would not see him. He stared at the floor in order not to attract attention to himself.

The wreath of dried flowers had fallen on the floor, and in a groove of the pedestal of a pillar clung some hard candle wax. The candles in the brass candlesticks illuminated the image of Santa Barbara with the raised arms. Her attitude was like that of the green mermaid in one of the patios on Payande. But different, thought Carlos Arturo. The gesture of the playful little mermaid had become meaningless in the dried-up fountain.

Santa Barbara in her gilded niche raised her arms protectively. She was the patron saint of the old house and had been since the time of the Spaniards, since the time of the former inhabitants who had fled. Last night he thought she had a defensive rather than a protective appearance. Now the thought dawned on him that there could be still another interpretation.

His heart began to beat wildly. Again he looked at the pillar with the gray drops of candle wax in the hollow of the wood, and then stealthily, at Doña Isabel's room.

The old woman had raised herself partially and clasped the hand of Don Belisario. "But she *was* here last night," she repeated urgently. "No one will believe me, but she was here again!"

Yes, she had been here again! He had seen her, standing in the great room, between Doña Isabel's room and the altar. He had seen her for a split second in the blue glare of lightning before she vanished.

Hesitatingly he stretched out his hand to the pillar.

His fingers slid along the carved wood, along the vines and clusters of leaves. Over the heavy bunches of grapes, through the deep grooves between the vines, along the underside of a curled leaf. He felt it click under his fingertips. The panel moved. Between the pillars the image of Santa Barbara in her scalloped niche slowly receded. A musty smell met him. The candles flickered and went out. He stared at the small dark opening, at the steps of a crumbling winding staircase that lost itself in the darkness between the thick walls.

In the room behind him it was very quiet. Then there were footsteps and confused voices.

Soledad began to wail, "Ave María, what is this? What is happening to us? Virgen Santísima!"

The frail, tired voice of Doña Isabel spoke, "What is it, Soledad? What are you doing? What is happening?"

The heavy step of Don Belisario came near, the floor creaking under his weight. "What is happening here?" he said harshly. "Out of the way, you two."

Carlos Arturo and Soledad stepped back. For a moment Don Belisario studied the small opening behind the altar attentively. Then he wriggled his big body through it and descended a few steps. They heard him shuffle about in the dark. Before long he appeared again. For the second time he examined everything, and then he looked at Carlos Arturo. "Did you discover this? How did you know? How did you figure it out?" he asked.

Carlos Arturo shrugged his shoulders. "I don't know," he said. "Perhaps by the candle wax on the pillar, or because I, too, knew that Ana-Amanda was here last night." He fell silent, casting a confused glance at the half-turned niche in which Santa Barbara raised her arms. Protectively? Defensively? Or was she beckoning?

Don Belisario wasn't listening to Carlos Arturo anymore. He slowly let the panel turn back. He made Carlos Arturo demonstrate how to open it. To Soledad he said, "Go and fetch a few of the hands and bring some light."

Soledad hastily shuffled off, and Don Belisario went to sit beside Doña Isabel's bed. "A secret passage, behind the altar," he said musingly. "The old colonial houses often have them, and Ana-Amanda knew about this one."

The old woman nodded absently. "She knows much, and she is very wicked," she said listlessly. "Raúl often has warned me against her."

There was the sound of heavy footsteps. Soledad returned with some workers and two lighted lamps.

Slowly they descended one behind the other. Don Belisario led with a lamp; the workers came close behind. Carlos Arturo followed them with pounding heart through the long, musty passage. He already knew where it would end.

21

They did not immediately recognize the place where the passage ended. They stood among piles of stone and heaped-up earth, with the clammy wind in their faces. Ana-Amanda's hut had been washed away, swept off with silt and boulders from the stone ridge. The bushes were buried in mud.

With difficulty they dug themselves a way through the mounds of earth, past uprooted shrubs, and across stretches of rock. The narrow paths had been blocked, and the big boulders were half buried in the mud. A few planks were sticking out of the rubbish, and they found a caldron, and, wedged between the boulders, the coffin.

"Ana-Amanda's hut . . ." muttered the farmhands. They glanced fearfully around. They looked at the opening between the rocks from which they had come out and then at the deep scar in the stone ridge where the earth had come down. They stood huddled together.

Don Belisario joined them. "Wasn't this Ana-Amanda's hut?" he asked.

The men nodded nervously. Don Belisario looked at the black earth and gray piles of rock that had poured like lava over the land . . . from the stone ridge to the edge of the lake. Branches and roots of trees protruded like angular arms. Don Belisario's one eye lighted on the coffin.

"Well," he said, "she won't need that anymore."

The men were silent, fidgeting uneasily. At last one of them said, "Perhaps she wasn't home."

"What do you mean?"

"Maybe she went up the mountains," the man repeated.

The others nodded. "Of course, she must have gone to the mountains before it happened."

"She knows everything. She sees things."

"Yes, she foresees the future. She must have known about it and left for the mountains. She'll come back."

Involuntarily they looked toward the mountains, now hidden by clouds. The wind began to blow over the lake. The water had risen high in the reeds. It was dark among the bushes and the big trees.

Carlos Arturo slipped away quietly, without saying

good-bye. He waded through the mud and debris in the direction of Payande. He saw a dead calf floating by with swollen belly, feet in the air. Vultures circled around and settled on it.

Some cows walked ahead of him, ponderously, with clumsy gait, horned heads held high, instinctively seeking higher ground. They crowded together in the road.

It began to rain again.

Wet through, Carlos Arturo reached Payande. People stood gathered in the yard, under the roof of a shed or leaning against the walls of an outbuilding. Some had a few pieces of furniture with them, others a chicken, a rabbit, or a bundle of clothing. Someone came walking through the mud holding a big, black umbrella. Children cried; dogs slunk about yelping. A few big boys were beating off snakes that had also come fleeing from the valley.

Carlos Arturo left mud tracks on the floor of the house as he entered. Doña Luisa and Transito came running when they heard him.

"Thank God, you're back," said his mother with a sigh of relief.

"And muddy from top to toe, poor fellow," said Transito. "I'll tell the maids to get some water ready in the bathroom." She shuffled off hastily.

"I stayed at Santa Barbara. The jeep is stuck, and I couldn't get back."

"That's what I thought, but we were anxious all the same. It's been a very bad night. The thunderstorm and such awful rains, everything underwater, and those poor people in the yard. We've been busy all night."

Transito came back. "There are pails of water in the bathroom," she said.

"I'll put out dry clothes for you, and I'll fetch your bathrobe and towels. Remember to dry yourself well," said Doña Luisa anxiously.

With his bathrobe and towels over his arm Carlos Arturo went to the bathroom. He took off his clothes, rinsed the mud from his body, and soaped himself twice. Big globs of suds fell on the cracked cement floor at his feet. He scooped the cool rainwater out of the pails with a pan and poured it over his body. Then, rubbed warm and dry and wrapped in his bathrobe, he walked to his room. Slowly he put on dry clothes that had been laid out on the bed for him. He began to feel a little better, calmer and less strained, though he still was tired after his long, wakeful night at Santa Barbara.

His mother was sitting at the table in the dining room. With hands clasped nervously, she looked at a corner of the ceiling, where a damp spot had spread alarmingly. The drops welled from the cracks and splashed into the buckets. It leaked in more and more places. They could hear the irritating music of water dripping into pans, cans, and pails all over the house.

Transito entered with steaming coffee. "Here," she said to Carlos Arturo. "Drink this. It will do you good." She lingered, looking at him while he drank his coffee as if there was something that she wanted to say and she did not know how. She and Doña Luisa exchanged meaningful glances.

Carlos Arturo knew that they both were waiting for him to say something, but he did not feel like answering a lot of questions about Doña Isabel and his stay at Santa Barbara. He didn't want to talk yet. So he sat silently, warming his hands around the cup, his head bent.

At last Transito said, "Did the *señora* tell you that Carmencita has a daughter?"

"Yes, Carmencita has a daughter," Doña Luisa repeated automatically.

"Sabas is furious with Carmencita. He scolded her, he called her all sorts of names, and now he is sulking." Transito shook her head. "I don't know what's going to become of us all, so many problems, one after the other!"

Doña Luisa got up. She began to pace the room. She moved a pail under one of the leaks and wrung out a mop. She walked to the kitchen where the maids were cooking soup in big pots. Transito followed her, and Carlos Arturo heard her mutter, "We've enough problems. That's certain."

When it cleared a bit, Carlos Arturo had the horses

saddled and went to look at the cattle with Juan de la Cruz and Sabas. Venetië was completely underwater. The cattle had broken through the fences and had escaped to the far side of the mountains. They were lowing unhappily. Some of them had been hurt. Scraps of bloody hide still clung to the trampled barbed wire. Vultures floated on the swollen bodies of drowned cattle. Their beaks tore at the bloated flesh.

The water from the little rivers cascaded from the mountains, yellow, hissing water that foamed over the rocks. The three men returned single file through the flooded fields, somber and silent. Carlos Arturo brought up the rear.

The rest of the day crawled past. It grew dark early and began to rain again.

Carlos Arturo went around the grounds several times. He talked with the men who sat huddled together. They stared resignedly at the rain falling in streams. He stopped at the big shed to talk with the woman who cooked for the farmhands. She looked ill-tempered.

"There's no end to the work, with so many people," she complained, as she slowly and unwillingly stirred the food in the big pots.

"They're busy in the kitchen too," said Carlos Arturo. "It's lucky we just stocked up on new provisions."

The woman did not answer, but someone else said,

"Juan de la Cruz's wife killed a pigeon for Carmencita. I saw her drop the blood into a pan with corn mush. Warm, sweet corn mush for Carmencita. She needs the warmth of life after her delivery."

"They won't be able to leave for a while," said another woman. "Carmencita can't cross water. That's unlucky for the first forty days. She can't even cross a bridge."

Against the wall of one of the outbuildings Sabas's mother hung crookedly in her chair. The children slid past her into the building and pressed around Carmencita and the baby. Carlos Arturo could not bring himself to go in and see the child.

He went back to the big house, which was now quite dark. His mother, Transito, and the servants were busy. The lamps hadn't been brought yet. He stood on the veranda. As he watched the rain dripping from the trees on the lawn he thought of the talk he had heard about Carmencita. Carmencita and the warmth of life. The warmth of life and the chill of death. Those two concepts embodied the extremes; in between lay all the gradations of illness and discomfort. His father always had been irritated by the superstitious beliefs of his people.

Carmencita was forbidden to cross water, even over a bridge, for forty days. So Sabas would stay for that time too, and the realization made him feel uncomfortable. He distrusted Sabas. This afternoon he had taken care that Sabas rode ahead of him. He made sure that his back was never turned to Sabas. He knew his behavior was irrational. He had been alone with Sabas and nothing had happened. Nor could he accuse Sabas of anything. He had no proof. Only the three names on El Cojo's crate. Again he wondered what these three men could have had against his father and which of them had conceived the plan.

It was late when his mother finally appeared. On the grounds it was nearly quiet. "A few children got ill," she said, when they finally sat at the table. "I did what I could, but we haven't much medicine."

"No," agreed Carlos Arturo. He thought of his father's dispensary. The stuff there would be mostly unusable. Still, he'd go there tomorrow and take a look at it.

Steps sounded in the hall, and Juan de la Cruz appeared at the door. He took off his hat. "Would the *señora* have some bandages?" he asked.

"Bandages?"

"Two men had a fight in the shed, with machetes," said Juan de la Cruz.

Doña Luisa and Carlos Arturo looked at each other. They shoved back their chairs simultaneously.

"Where?" asked Doña Luisa.

"Back of the kitchen, *señora*," said Juan de la Cruz.

In the kitchen door stood a man with a faded shirt half covering his shoulder. The empty sleeve was torn and red with blood. In his upper arm he had a deep flesh wound. Groups of men stood behind him in the rain.

"Come in and sit there," said Doña Luisa. "Bring boiled water," she told the two maids who stood gaping curiously.

Carlos Arturo entered the big kitchen with a bottle of iodine, alcohol, and a package of sterile gauze. "That's all I could find," he said.

"Bandages," said his mother, while she began to wash the wound carefully. "I need bandages and cotton."

Carlos Arturo ran outside again, past the curious faces in the doorway.

"Ai, ai," someone complained. "What a thing to happen when Ana-Amanda isn't here!"

"No, Ana-Amanda is away in the mountains, they say."

"When will she be back?"

"Who can say, with all this rain?"

They kept elbowing one another at the door.

Carlos Arturo strode to the small dispensary behind the chapel. He searched in the cupboard among the pots with dried-out ointment and tubes with spoiled vitamins and pills. In a big tin he found bandages and rolls of cotton. He also took out an old rusty pair of scissors.

When he came back, his mother was daubing the wound.

She smiled at the scissors and bandaged the wound. "I don't need the cotton after all, Carlos Arturo," she said. "Put all that back where you found it." Then she said to the man, "Try to keep your arm up as much as possible, do you hear?"

"Yes, *señora*," he said meekly.

Carlos Arturo took the rest of the bandages and the cotton back to the dispensary, replacing them carefully where he had found them. For a moment he lingered. The small room with the methodically arranged medicines, now useless, looked pathetic. Tomorrow he would come and clean everything.

He made his last circuit of the grounds. In Carmencita's room people were talking. He heard the voices of Sabas and his old mother. Her big chair stood before the door. The light of his lantern played over the coarse wood and the white rawhide. He stood still and bent over it. He looked attentively at the white horsehide with the little brown spots. He stroked it several times with the palm of his hand, as if he could not believe it. But it was true!

Trembling with excitement he ran to the study. He sat down before the desk and took out the package of photographs. There, behind the big zebu bull El Gigante sat Sabas on his brown mottled horse. A brown mottled horse, irregularly marked, with a big white spot on the hindquarters that ran from the back all the way along the flanks and over the left hind leg. He sat for a long time with the photographs spread in front of him.

"Sabas's horse. Don't sit on it," the old woman had called once from her chair on the veranda. "Sabas's horse."

Now, at last he was really certain.

22

He sat for a long time in the silent study with the lamp and the photographs on the desk. Gnats hummed around the light. The rain fell steadily. The leak in the corner over the bookcase dripped regularly.

Edelio and Jacinto and Sabas, on his mottled horse, of which he had glimpsed the white hindquarters. His father had gone outside and found men he had known and trusted. They must have muttered something about the cattle, about a sick cow. Or they might have said that someone had had an accident—Santos, perhaps, or El Cojo. Then his father would not have been suspicious as they led him to the mountains, to El Cojo's hut. He was with people he knew, men who had worked for him for years. No, he would not have suspected them, not until it was too late.

Carlos Arturo got up with a jerk. He paced the

room. But why? Who had thought of such a monstrous scheme? He stood at the table with the untidy heap of old books that he had rescued from the corner of the bookcase. Absently he stacked them. Small stacks, the spines all on the same side. They felt clammy. As he opened them to let them dry, he saw some underlined paragraphs, and here and there he saw a note in his father's rapid, forceful script. He tried to decipher the blotted letters.

"A narcotic drink, made of seven seeds of the tonga, used for illegal purposes." And under that: "Twenty drops are the equivalent of sixty milligrams opium." Between brackets was a scribble saying, "See Dr. Waring." The name of Dr. Waring had been underlined in another one of the books too. Now he took the books up and leafed through them.

Most of them, he saw, were about medicinal plants. The name *datura* was underlined everywhere, and after *Datura sanguinea* his father had put in parentheses the word *tonga*. In the book by Pardal he saw the word *witch tree* underlined three times.

He fetched a chair and began to read the underlined passages with attention. In the back of a book called *Magical Plants* he found a little, much-thumbed pamphlet. It had been written in 1892 by a doctor in Cauca, Ricardo Escobar. *The Tonga and Its Magic Effects* was the title.

Always that name *tonga*. *Datura sanguinea,* a shrub with pink cuplike flowers. The shrubs around the hut of Ana-Amanda!

The word *witch tree, arbol de bruja,* underlined three times. "A narcotic drink, made of seven seeds of the tonga, used for illegal purposes!" Impatiently he leafed through the books until he found the passage again. The blotted letters. His father's handwriting!

His father had known of the dark practices of Ana-Amanda. He had warned Doña Isabel against her. He had tried to free the people around Laguna Grande of her influence, of the spell that she had over them!

But his efforts had been in vain. Ana-Amanda had known all the time that his father wanted to undermine her power, and carefully she had planned her revenge! Edelio, thought Carlos Arturo bitterly, Edelio with his batch of ailing children. And Jacinto, the son of old Santos, who never left off discussing his impending death. Sabas's mother, who had been an invalid for years.

Edelio, Jacinto, and Sabas! They must have trod the narrow winding path around the lake toward the hut of Ana-Amanda often. And Ana-Amanda gave them medicine and brewed her potions. She listened to them patiently and helped them again and again. She bided her time, and one night she issued her orders. And they obeyed.

She had made no mistake, with the exception of El Cojo perhaps. El Cojo, who had lost his leg. Maybe she wanted to include El Cojo, and he had refused. Or maybe he had not dared to refuse directly but tried instead to stop the plan in his own way.

"Yes, *señor*, the rainy season begins soon. It would be best before the rainy season. . . ." But his father hadn't understood. Or perhaps he thought that he need not fear Ana-Amanda, that his influence was greater than hers. Perhaps he had been smiling when El Cojo disappeared into the darkness.

Carlos Arturo shivered. He pushed the books away from him. The door opened, and Transito entered.

"I saw light," she said. "Are you still sitting here?" She looked attentively at him. For one moment he was tempted to tell Transito what he suspected, but he repressed the impulse. She would not want to be confronted with the revelation. She would not want to know. Her opinion was that of the people around the Laguna Grande, the people who believed in Ana-Amanda and feared her.

Transito kept looking at him. At last she said, "I'll make you some more coffee." She shuffled off and came back a moment later with the coffee. She watched him while he sipped it slowly. She lingered, just as she had done that afternoon, as if she wanted to say something.

"It keeps raining," she said.

"Yes, it keeps raining," agreed Carlos Arturo.

"Those poor people who live around the lake all have fled from the water. Many are here now on Payande."

"Yes."

"And the hut of Ana-Amanda has been washed away, they tell me."

"Yes, with a landslide. I've seen it."

Transito waited to see if he was going to say anything more. When he remained silent, she continued speaking. "They say that Ana-Amanda has been seen in the mountains." She waited again, looking at Carlos Arturo. "But who can say with all this rain!"

Carlos Arturo met her eyes. "She was at Santa Barbara last night."

"At Santa Barbara?"

"Yes, I saw her. I thought at first she was Doña Isabel."

"Oh," said Transito.

"She often went to Santa Barbara at night to visit Doña Isabel. There's a passage leading from her hut to the Santa Barbara house with a secret entrance behind the altar. Even Doña Isabel didn't know about it, only Ana-Amanda."

Transito nodded. She did not seem surprised. "Ana-Amanda knew everything," she said. "She knew the house well."

"What do you mean? Why did she know the house well?" His fingers touched the books before him on the table.

"She used to live there as a child," said Transito. He looked at her with startled eyes.

"Yes, she lived there as a child," Transito went on. "She was born there. Perhaps her mother showed her the passage, or perhaps she discovered it herself. Who shall say? The mother of Ana-Amanda came from the Cauca. She was a wise woman. All Ana-Amanda knew of healing plants and looking into the future she learned from her mother. Her mother was cook on Santa Barbara, and Ana-Amanda was born there. When Don Fausto married, he sent her away."

"They didn't go back to the Cauca?" asked Carlos Arturo, to fill a pause.

"No they didn't return to the Cauca. They built the hut near the stone ridge where Ana-Amanda lived, first with her mother, then alone."

"Did Don Fausto know?"

"Of course he knew. He always looked after her. He left her a quarter of his estate after he died. That's the way Don Fausto was, hard but just."

Carlos Arturo was silent. He tried to remember what Doña Isabel had said about her father, Don Fausto, who had continued to look after Ana-Amanda and had left her a quarter of his estate.

Slowly the realization came to him what that conduct implied.

"Then . . ." he began.

"Exactly." Transito nodded. "She was his daughter. They were very alike; they had the same character."

"And a fourth of Santa Barbara belongs to Ana-Amanda?"

"More now, I think, for Ana-Amanda bought a lot of land in the course of the years. She was a very proud woman, even though she lived simply. She didn't want to be less than her half sister. And, as I was saying, she was much more like her father than Doña Isabel."

"I see," said Carlos Arturo, toying with the books on the table. "I see."

"The people around the lake always respected Don Fausto, and they always respected Ana-Amanda."

"Yes," said Carlos Arturo.

"Who knows where she is now? *Dios mio*. Where could she be, with all this rain? Who knows when she'll be back?" Transito sighed, took the empty cup, and left the room.

Carlos Arturo sat for a while without moving. Finally he got up quietly, took the lamp, and walked through the silent house to his mother's room. He hesitated a moment and then cautiously opened the door. The light from the lamp fell inside.

"Mother. . . ."

"What is it, Carlos Arturo?" said his mother wearily from the big bed.

"That land that was sold. . . . Who bought it? Was it Doña Isabel or was it Ana-Amanda?"

There was a pause. "Couldn't we talk about that tomorrow, Carlos Arturo? It's late, and I'm tired. You're tired too."

"Yes, but Mother. . . ."

"You must go to sleep now, Carlos Arturo. Your Uncle Ernesto settled it all. He had a power of attorney."

Carlos Arturo lifted his hand with the lamp; the light glided farther into the room. His mother's face was a dark spot against the pillow.

"But you found that power of attorney later, when . . . when my father wasn't here anymore!"

"Yes . . . well . . . I'm not sure. Your father never told me anything about his affairs. You know that."

"But he loved the land; he loved Payande. He never would have agreed to sell any of it!"

She made a discouraged gesture. "There was no other solution. We needed the money. The workers had to be paid and so did your school bills. There were taxes and debts to the bank. And now the death duties have to be paid, and we still haven't cleared the tenure of the estate. You know that. Nothing has been settled."

He stood very still. The lamp began to waver and smoke. No, he thought bitterly, nothing is settled.

What would he do about the damage caused by the rain: the cattle that were drowned, the leaks in the old dilapidated house?

And what about all those people, driven from the valley, who had come and sought refuge on Payande? Payande, to which he had returned, elated and full of expectations. Payande, which he loved, but which never again could be restored to that happy place of old they had known during the days when his father had been alive. The lamp flickered once more and went out.

"You must go to sleep now, Carlos Arturo. It's late."

"Yes, it's late," he agreed. "But it's stopped raining."

They listened. It was true. It was not raining anymore.

Slowly Carlos Arturo walked through the dark, silent house to his room. For a long time he stood at the dark window. Sounds reached him, sounds carried on the wind: noises in the yard, a grumbling, sleepy voice, a suppressed exclamation, the whining of a dog. From the lakeshore came the cry of a night bird, and from farther off the deep roar of the Río Tigre.

It was very dark, but the rain had stopped.

Siny R. van Iterson was born in the Netherlands Antilles, on the island of Curaçao, and has traveled extensively. For short periods she has lived in many different places, including Europe, the United States, Central and South America, and the Caribbean. Interested in writing from her earliest years, she first worked on a newspaper and later began to write children's books. She lives, with her husband and their four children, in Bogotá, Colombia.

Mrs. van Iterson is the author of a number of books published in Holland. Several of them have been translated into German and Danish.